The Pitfall Experiments:
ALPHA

VAUGHN FEIGHAN

CRANTHORPE.
MILLNER

A CIP catalogue record for this title is available from the British Library.

First published (2020)

ISBN 978-1-912964-14-7 (Paperback)

www.cranthorpemillner.com

Cranthorpe Millner Publishers

Inspired by, and dedicated to, the real-life
Colman, Molly, and Kendall.

Perfection is artificial. Do *not* be perfect.

CHAPTER 1

My active heartrate is five beats slower than that of an Alaskan sled dog – when it's sleeping. My eyesight is sharper than that of a bald eagle. Like a bloodhound on the trail of an escaped convict, the smell of death and betrayal greets me at every turn, but unlike the dog, my bite is much worse than my bark. The only thing on this planet that has the ability to outwit, outsmart or destroy me is me; I am a carnal animal, a perfect machine, and a Famous Alpha Spike.

My name is Colman Cai and I'm Famous because I was born for death.

I enjoy being Famous, but I despise the people who made me Famous. All the same, I adore the people who *keep* me Famous.

This whole thing – my life – is a show for those people who have propelled me to the top of the artificial food chain. My purpose is strictly entertainment and the fact that I can be Executed at any moment is my reality. The people I destroy are my legacy but enjoying the life of the rich and powerful is worth it.

Honestly, I do not care about any of this; it is how it has always been…and will always be.

Each day, an escort of four midnight-black Cadillac Escalades arrive outside my penthouse at 220 Central Park South between 8:05 AM and 9:25 AM. The cars arrive sporadically because the horde of fans crowded outside my building have an uncanny ability to detect when I am about to move. Their desperate cheers float from the ground, past the sixty-nine floors, and I know the cars have arrived when their cheers turn into hysterical screams.

Once the first car has confirmed its arrival, I receive a notification on my EYE – my technologically superior communication platform embedded in my cornea – alerting me that my personal security has exited the transport and is coming to collect me. It takes them approximately four to six minutes to exit the cars, sweep the lobby, then ascend to the penthouse. I named these guards Cassidy, Rosen, Downey, and Fanto. I always choose to give my staff fake names because they would be in severe danger should I know their real identities. Anyone who gets close to me always dies.

As I wait for them, my stylist team – a thick-accented Jamaican woman, whom I call Bella, and a man from the Czech Republic, whom I call Roberto – work feverously to make me presentable. As Bella and Roberto comb my hair, pluck my eyebrows, add a smidge of makeup to my cheeks, I scroll through my EYE to update myself on the morning news. They do this as I sit in a massive, leather-backed chair in front of a mammoth mirror with lights around it. It reminds me of the kind I saw in an old-time Western movie …

not that you should know what that is. The world has been stripped of all popular forms of art, but I am one of the lucky ones who has access to historical artefacts. Money buys me that privilege.

By the time I finish checking my EYE, my security will have cleared the lobby. The screaming fans are herded, like animals, to metal pens outside my building. My loyal team is required to wear matching Hugo Boss suits so that they look professional. Hugo Boss sponsored me when I was a young Spike, and now the company owns a piece of me; I must return their investment by wearing their clothes. Every member also wears sunglasses with their suits because, come on, how could they not? No one takes security seriously unless they're wearing dark shades.

As my guards make their way to collect me from the penthouse, the adoring fans start to shake the metal barriers they are huddled against in anticipation. People tend to lose themselves in my presence. The building staff make sure that my exit is cleared, and security begins their daily routine.

The elevator takes only thirty seconds to ascend the sixty-nine floors and my team always arrive in the same way: Fanto and Rosen out first, Downey and Cassidy following behind. The regularity comforts me. These four were assigned to me when I was first created for the Pit and have been with me ever since. They've saved my life multiple times.

No. They've saved my Image multiple times, which is kind of the same thing.

"Mr. Cai, it is time to go," Fanto says once they emerge from the golden-plated elevators. "The lobby has been cleared. The staff is awaiting our instructions. We pulled the vehicles around back by the boarding dock today. There were more Sivs crowded in front of the main entrance this morning than we had anticipated. Our drivers have assured me that the boarding dock has been blocked and secured for departure. We are waiting for your orders. No hurry, sir."

I always remember to thank Bella and Roberto for their work while admiring myself in the mirror. Thirty seconds later, my vintage Louis Vuitton jacket, Armani aviator sunglasses, Tumi backpack, and a simple baseball hat are in my possession and I am leaving the safety of my home to enter the world of the dying. Fanto signals one of the other three guards to accompany me on my descent and Bella and Roberto look towards me as the elevator doors close. I know exactly what they think each time I flash them my award-winning smile as the doors close on me. Likely, I will be back tonight to do this all over again, but there is a chance this may be my finale.

The descent takes twenty seconds and I practice my smile. Fanto holds a mirror in front of me because he understands how crucial this simple task is to my survival. My smile can melt the hearts of the people I meet or be the final thing they see before I send them to their deaths. The Keepers ripped all my teeth out at ten years old and replaced with a perfect set of fake ones to ensure I would always have a picture-perfect smile so that they would also get a return on their investment. The longer I stay alive, the more money they make. Fanto places the mirror back in his jacket and my pseudo-emotions are officially prepped for whatever is to come.

Walking out of the elevator, I am greeted by flashing cameras, waving hands, pens and paper thrust in my face, wails of joy, and the rattling of the metal barricades outside from those who could not get back in. In the southwest corner of the lobby rests my camera crew, or as I like to call them, my SQUAD.

The lead cameraman reaches for the button to broadcast my position to the world and my calm demeanor ignites at the very same moment. This single red light means money, Fame, power, luxury, isolation, resilience, and Execution. At this point, my security is trailing behind me so to give me space to interact with the Sivs – the regular, non-Spike citizens. They are whispering into their earpieces as they begin their surveillance of the crowded and noisy lobby. I re-watch the tapes of my morning entrance sometimes and it would not be unusual to see my security smirk as they walk behind me. Everyone loves Fame.

I quickly pass through the waves of people and sign exactly twenty autographs and take four pictures. I wrap my arms around the shoulders of Sivs from across the Country to make it seem like my gesture is authentic. After I am done with these pathetic, risible necessities, my security team escorts me to the boarding dock where we load into the cars for whatever destination has been planned. Around this time every morning, I am greeted by one of my longest relationships and number one supporter: Molly. Molly has been in my life since my Entrance Day on April 19th and she is a combination of publicist, gatekeeper, promoter, and make-shift handler. Each day she waits there and smiles with a mouth full of teeth that no one in this world could possibly replicate.

"Hey beautiful, would you like to hear what I have planned for you today?" Molly says, tucking a lock of silver hair into her flawless bun.

I smile and give her the most seductive grin I can mimic. It took me almost four years to master the seductive look but now it is officially programmed into my vast array of replicated emotion [Eyes: Lower. Eyelids: Lower. Mouth Corners: Draw Upward. Right Eyebrow: Raise. Chin: Lower. Lips: Slight Pucker. Execute.] One would think that this would become tiresome, but Molly blushes every day and it reaffirms that she has faith in my ability to charm and Execute. In my life, it is rare to have someone so devoted to my physical well-being and so entrenched in my non-televised life. Normally, Sivs only see what you want them to see. We see from where we stand. Molly, on the other hand, is monitoring me all the time. She knows everything that happens in my life. The security guards continue to push me forward while Molly trots next to the human shield that has since formed back around me. High heels clicking, she yells the agenda for the day.

"Colman, we have you arriving at the tarmac in approximately 41 minutes which will leave you a whole ten minutes to decompress before we will have to get the shot of you walking onto your jet. You are going to pull into Terminal P because that is where your jet landed this morning. I want you to take and post four pictures between the time you taxi until the time you land ... can you do this for me?"

"Anything for you, Molly," I grumble.

"Perfect, okay, so once we land in London we will head to Buckingham Palace where you will be greeted by Marist and Vassar, the queen's granddaughters. You have met them before, do you remember? They are still angry with you from when you set their grandmother's hair on fire but I worked my magic and was assured they would be there to greet you so it does not hurt your Image. When you land, remember to make sure that your shirt is buttoned down at least three ..."

The minute clothing is mentioned, it signals the end of my personal responsibility because I have a team of people in charge of that already. My hair is gelled to the right side because my team of neuroscientists says that this is more of an accepted style in London. My eyebrows have been slimmed for the same reason. There is a small injection of lip gel that keeps my lips flat and smooth. I cannot look too overjoyed but also not too disengaged. I have a Henley on, and two buttons are unbuttoned. Rule of thumb: one button down is "just chilling", two buttons down is "sexy-time", three buttons down is "clothes come off". Every part of my being is curated to that last detail.

I am perfect in every way. My pectorals are outlined just right in these shirts which is why they are my favorite. My Regulation size is a 38.5" chest with a half an inch fluctuation in either direction. When the wind blows, you can see the outline of my eight pack - my pride and joy.

As we breeze through the back entrances of the building, I see the cars waiting near the boarding dock and feel my scalp prickle ever so slightly … my job is about to begin.

I know it before anybody else senses that something is wrong. The brief sinking feeling in my stomach is suddenly replaced with an injection of pure adrenaline, making my entire field of vision crystalize. Molly is still moving her mouth, but no noise is coming out and I tap my ears to physically bring them back to attention. My security team is scanning the perimeter, but the camera crew is getting too close to my guards and they are getting anxious. That is never a good sign.

Confirming my suspicion, one of the crew members yells something behind me and Rosen is the first to turn, immediately tensing and alerting the other three members of my team. From somewhere in the back, a golden egg strikes one of the crew members in the back of the head and immediately penetrates his skull, burrowing deeper and deeper into his brain.

[Alert. Weapon Detected.] He crumples, the camera falls, and everyone but my security team instantly scatters. The remaining videographers scurry to various positions in the loading bay to capture my next moves. Adrenaline surges, my heart starts pounding in my ears, my fingers are tingling, and I have serious cottonmouth.

My EYE flashes red and I jump out of the way as another golden egg comes careening my way. I scan the open area of floor and begin my expert assessment. [Area Cleared. One Execution. Lookup (golden, eggs, brain, death, airborne, catapult). Execute.] My EYE computes this information and within .02 milliseconds, returns a positive match for a biological weapon nicknamed "Screaming Chicken". Two more eggs come streaming my way, but my EYE goes dark, leaving me with a clear view of the scene in front of me. Two men in grey suits come streaking across the lobby towards me. [Assessment. Options. Strategy (men, grey, two, two-hundred pounds, biological weapon).] With a threat now visible, as per regulation, my security team abandons me.

The first Encounter of the day is underway. I do not need to look at the results from my EYE to know what I should do. I see a brief glimpse of the "Options" and "Recommendations" tabs before the EYE once again goes blank. I have faced much worse than a weapon called a Screaming Chicken. I swing my athletic 6'2", 170-pound frame up and over the bay doors and plaster myself against the ceiling, waiting for these two meatheads to try their luck against me. They are no real danger to me. I spring on them only when they are directly under me.

The men enter my space, then I drop right on top of them like a jaguar stalking a gazelle. As I freefall from the ceiling, I savor the moment. This is what gives me purpose and keeps me Famous. Life moves in slow motion. The infrared beams of hotel security cameras frantically scan the entire area, no doubt with Molly behind the production of this frenzy, searching to film the Encounter. If done correctly, my Profile will get boosted from these Executions. My sunglasses fall free and I quickly bite off the tip and plunge the sharp blade into the first man's neck. He crumbles and awkwardly reaches behind him to grasp the makeshift blade. I have severed his cervical vertebrae; he will die almost immediately.

The second man turns around and snarls at me. He glances at his flailing partner and yanks something from his jacket. Without looking at what his weapon is, I snatch my hat off my head and blow the reservoir of white powder in his face. He starts screaming and before I know it, both men are on the floor laying open-eyed with blood dripping from the corners of their mouths. I gather myself and make sure I grab my Armani shades out of the man's neck and baseball hat off the floor. It is not necessary to turn on my EYE, I know this brief Encounter was captured and is being live-streamed. I relax as my beaming security team praises me while the videographers emerge from their poorly lit hiding places. I place my hat on my head, my

[10]

sunglasses on my face, then take my mirror out of my backpack. I adjust the collar of my jacket and wipe the spit and blood off my face.

Molly comes prancing back out a moment later screaming, "Colman! It is not even 9 AM and our team already has something to broadcast! Okay, someone please move these bodies and take care of that poor cameraman. We will make sure to alert his family right away. Wait! Get a good shot of their faces ... and the blood. Zoom in right on the puncture mark in his neck ... yes, very good. Get a close-up of the boils on the second one's face. Great! Let's board the cars everybody."

Everything goes back to normal. My security team retake their positions around me, looking for unwarranted and unplanned Siv interaction. The camera crew rejoins me from a distance and the reporters – who constantly magically appear out of thin air – selected to be in the docket for the day start the round of questions that traditionally happens after every Encounter.

"Colman!"

"How did you see that coming?"

"How did you decide what maneuvers to do?"

"What did you have for breakfast?"

"Who are you wearing?"

"Did the designers make the sunglasses shank especially for you or did you make it yourself?"

"Do you know how much money you have made this morning?"

The noise is a buzz. They all just yell over each other.

Molly has started discussing the agenda again, my security team is holding open the doors to my Escalade while my SQUAD files into the remaining three cars. My EYE is blinking yellow with new messages from Producers and Keepers who now want to endorse me. As I board the truck, the oncoming ambulance noise instinctively brings a smile to my face. London is not ready for me.

CHAPTER 2

Welcome to my world of death: I Execute them as they try—and fail—to Execute me.

My Donors were selected by the Country for the post-war lifestyle of "Spike for Siv". The Country thought it was a good idea to fabricate two unequal classes of people to avoid internal conflict. This was so we could create a new society of inter-dependent Beings; we would both receive some benefit by living with one another.

The Sivs are the Observing Class. They look like Spikes. They talk like Spikes. They act like Spikes. There is one significant difference: Sivs do not have my super awesome, ass-kicking, muscle building, gorgeous smile-wearing, boyish charm. They do not have it and the only way they can achieve it is by Executing me. Hence, I must strike first.

Today could be my Execution Day.

But probably not.

Sivs have been marked, chipped, and are told to reproduce regularly. They get diseases, they are required to make these things called "children", and they are allowed to die on their own. A Siv is what every Being was like before the attack. They are an ordinary, self-governing body that has strong tendencies to clump together to create things called "families". A family is a collection of Sivs that live together or in proximity to one another. They engage in an Encounter that is called Love.

If two Sivs partake in Love, then they will move into a house or an apartment together. After two Sivs have lived with each other for five years, they are required to apply for a Permit to create a child. Once the Country approves the original Permit, they are then required to apply for a Permit every three years until the government tells them to stop. The Country regulates this process to make sure that our population does not dwindle to lower figures than we already have. You see, I need an audience. Without Sivs, my purpose would be obsolete. Without a show pony, there can be no show.

Spikes are different. Spikes are a species of Being who cannot die naturally, feel no physical pain, are not allowed to have "children" and are hunted on a daily basis for the viewing pleasure of others. My species was designed in a lab by Keepers –scientists who know the inner desires of Sivs. Keepers are part of the highest functioning levels of the Country and are old-world neuroscientists, psychologists, and sociologists who select desirable traits for the Spike production. These teams researched and defined characteristics from pre-war that were valued above all others.

There is a female Beta Spike in the south of the Country who has eyes that can see into your deepest desires. There is another Beta Spike in the West that has never been injured in an Encounter. There is another that can seduce any Spike or Siv, male or female. However, each of these players has their own distinct Pitfall. A Pitfall cannot be engineered out of a Spike's design. The female Spike in the south may be able to see into you but she Executes too many Sivs; she is distraught with the unfathomable weight which comes with truly understanding other Beings. Her Pitfall is knowledge. The Spike who can seduce anyone attracts them wherever he goes; he can never truly be alone. His Pitfall is possession.

That is why they are Beta Spikes.

But my Pitfall? Well, I don't have one. At least, I don't have one that I know of. That's what makes me an Alpha: the best of the best.

After the nuclear meltdown, famine, drought, large black clouds, and occasional life-destroying tumors became less common. The Country needed to give Sivs a reason to live. They allowed the familial structure to remain but quickly realized that although one should live and breathe to build familial relationships, many Sivs abandoned this notion after years of making children. They wanted a reason to continue existing for themselves, something that made them "happy". Happy is this concept that when you look at something and enjoy seeing it or enjoy feeling it, it makes your brain feel good. When your brain feels good, your body feels good. Sivs were not content with only having a family, so in the ALT Convention, Keepers built the first Spike.

Around 2025, a country – which is no longer in existence – launched a series of missile strikes in response to our Spike Program. Needless to say, or maybe it is important to say, this country was obliterated within four hours of the first missile striking the ground.

The Country in which I live – or America as it was once called – was previously composed of these things called States. There were fifty of them and they existed in happy unity with each other. They were very different to what we call States today. The Country absorbed everything around it. Things that were once called a country is now a State.

When our borders were breached, we released a series of biological and chemical compounds in retaliation. Unfortunately, these compounds were misused and obliterated half of the globe. There were nuclear meltdowns, famine, drought, disease, huge black clouds … you name it, it happened. In the wake of this disaster, the population of the Country turned inward and isolated itself from the rest of the world. Our infrastructure was not equipped to take care of this many people, so our Super – a dictatorial President – authorized the release of another strain on the weakest members of its own population.

After the Country had reduced the population to a mere 30 million members, it sought to rebuild from the ground up. Our current Super is a man named Kendall Khan. He is a ruthless dictator from the Democratic Republic of the Congo and although he is fifty to sixty years old, he only looks slightly older than me. The incredible aging technology that the Keepers created allows him to do this. He has been around since the first Encounter and my guess is that he will be around for the last.

An Encounter, by the way, is a purposeful attack orchestrated by Keepers. Sivs pay money to the government and the Keepers will approve or deny the Siv's request to attempt to Execute a Spike. If this sounds ridiculous, it should. If a Siv kills a Spike, then that Siv is supposedly rewarded with traits of that slain Spike. There is one catch: a Siv has never defeated an Alpha Spike. Nevertheless, the hope of doing so – achieving a life without financial or emotional worry – is the driving factor. It keeps me in business to say the least. The Pit is The Country's greatest pastime and the reason for existence.

How has this not bored people by now? I have no idea. You would think that most people would come to their senses after realizing not a single Alpha Spike has ever been Executed by a Siv. And yet, no one has. I am always getting new technology, coming up with new stunts, and live a life that is too good to be true. I am the epitome of their god and no one wants to look away from my blinding light – even if I am more of the devil.

Plus, there are 24/7 live broadcasts of each Spike's life. Every detail, every sneeze, every breath, every drop of sweat, every step – it's all recorded for Sivs' viewing pleasure. Photographers, videographers, social media accounts, they all exist to monitor my class of Being. I am on a screen almost every second of my day: when I shower, when I eat, when I travel, when I nap, et cetera. My antics to get away from my overbearing security team, as well as my banter with Molly, provide more viewing pleasure.

Other States, such as England, do not partake in the Pit, as they see it as cruel and unusual punishment to have someone on display on a daily basis. However, because the Country still maintains and develops the largest store of chemical and biological weapons, other States have allowed the continuance of the Spike Program in exchange for a weapons truce. The Country will not destroy them if they let us Execute each other. Fair, right? Not surprisingly, the other major governing bodies – Australia, England, Russia, France, Germany, Brazil, Canada, and China – make up a majority of Spike culture even though they say they hate what our government is doing. All over the globe, Sivs are locked into their screens scrolling through each player's profile.

I, of course, as the only Alpha left in the Country, am Numero Uno.

It might sound bad to be constantly on camera, but as I've said, participation in the Pit does come with its rewards. The price Sivs pay for an Encounter is more than enough to support my extravagant lifestyle. I fly in jets, party on yachts, pee in a golden toilet, and am super attractive. What else do I need in my life? Sivs have none of my abilities, none of my training … they are basically nothing compared to me.

Now that you know how I found myself in that Encounter this morning, as well as the operations of the Country and how it is protecting us, I want to give you a bit of a look inside me. As I said, my name is Colman Cai. My Entrance Day is April 19th, 2051, and I was created as an Alpha Spike. An Alpha Spike is the highest luxury you can get. Imagine if you were buying a car. You can go to a dealer and look around the lot to find a Ferrari that looks close to what you want, or you can go to the manufacturer and customize every last detail. Which would you pick? There are only three Alphas in Circulation today and I am the only one in the Country. The other two, one male and one female, have been captured and taken away for study – another hypocritical move by the other States.

Why are there only three of us? Well, simple. Betas are easy to create. Creation of an Alpha Spike requires an additional compound called Nalgene-521— an extra bit of insurance which makes me almost completely invincible. But the Country squandered all available resources while developing the Spike program, and it fell into short supply. According to what I've been told, I was one of the lucky last to receive it, and the first to survive and thrive with it. The Country has attempted to recreate the compound, but with no luck, so basically ... it's just me. Number One. The Best. The Only.

I was grown in a lab until ten years of maturity. On April 19th, 2051, my Tube was opened and out walked the incredibly handsome Spike who is speaking to you today. A Spike encompasses one of the Topics and sub-Topics that the Keepers value. This means I am handsome, strong, smart, educated, athletically gifted, socially praised, funny, and always smiling. My eyes are the color of the Arctic sky with gold specks. I have a Roman nose that fits my face with exactly the right specifications. I keep my hair trimmed neat. I make sure it is about an inch and a half to two inches on the top with a fade from a three into a one down the sides and around the back. The color fluctuates with the season. Each time I move, you can see the ripple of my forearms, pectorals, biceps, triceps, deltoids, abdominals, back muscles. My cheekbones look like they were shaped from granite and so does everything else. I Execute with precision and I even eat a burger with such passion that before you know it you want to take that burger off the screen and shove it onto your own face. Yeah, I am that good.

There is one minor point about Spikes that truly does not appeal to the rest of the world: we have no real emotions. That burger-eating passion? Manufactured, unfortunately. Initially, when the Keepers were in the experimentation phase of the program, they tried to facilitate the ability to emphasize and relate to Sivs and other Spikes. They wanted a more seamless transition between the two classes to ultimately make more money. During many, many

[20]

rounds of testing in the Pit, the first Alpha Spikes were unable to Execute because of the emotions they had developed in the process. They tried over and over again but after many trials and spending well over a billion dollars, they were unable to create a Spike that possessed any sort of regular emotion who was also willing to Execute another Being.

They discovered that Executing was a way of separating the soul from itself. If you divided the soul from itself, then you were unable to establish an identity. An identity is essential for survival. I talked to a few scientists after they had removed my amygdala nuclei – the emotional processing center of the brain – and they said I would be unable to feel pain in life, and (as a nice, final touch) the only way I would feel pleasure is when it came to Executing. Executing brings me pleasure. Surging adrenaline, hunting, killing … those are the only things that make me smile; when I'm under attack, my lips instinctively curve into one.

I still get dreams about my Entrance Day; the first and last time I felt any emotion. I remember walking out of my Tube while people in black lab coats shone lights in my eyes. Each of them was yelling numbers and vital signs but that is not what I remember the most. With fluid still draining around my ankles, I was fixated on the cameras. The red lights were everywhere but I was able to see through the glare. In a small room, protected by bullet-proof windows, I saw Kendall Khan standing next to two other people – all were observing me. These two other people were crying

– they must have been Sivs – and were holding onto one another. I do not know why, but I wanted to join them.

Seconds later, as I looked at the chaos, little silver balls were shot at me. They attached to different parts of my body and sent electrical signals into my muscles and brain. I vaguely remember looking back up to those tinted glass windows, wanting to go to those people I saw, to hold them, kiss them. Then my vision went dark and I woke up the next day, fully clothed, with a part of my brain missing. *They did this to me.*

And I felt nothing. No anger, no regret, no pity, nothing.

I was now a killer and meant to like it.

I absolutely do.

CHAPTER 3

As we approach Obama International Airport, there is a new set of camera crews waiting for me. They know the drill. Molly briefs me before I make any public comments and the rest of the posse begins to deboard the three Escalades that followed me. Molly starts talking as Fanto shuts the door.

"Colman, your performance was great, but maybe next time we can do a little better? In the past, you have had fifteen people attack you and this morning was only two. The strategy of biting your sunglasses into a shank will get you viewers but the powder you blew was a bit boring. The Keepers asked for more blood next time. We are trying to get the Press to report that the two men who attacked you were from a training program in Russia so that we can boost ratings."

"Won't be a problem. The media will report anything for that ratings boost," I mutter.

"Colman, don't be like that. You know your job, you know mine. Let's not forget that this is a team effort."

"What team effort? I only see myself in front of that camera. Did I miss someone? Did post-production crop someone out? Where is that other twenty-year-old that was born to kill?"

"Listen here. You know that I do not like playing the media's game any more than you do. I took this job because I wanted to protect you. There is no other reason for me to be here. I did not pick this life for you, and I know you did not pick this life for you. However, I am trying to make the best of it. So, let's put a smile on that face of yours and get out there for those cameramen! They have been waiting for the last fifty minutes."

"Okay. Where exactly am I going again today? Did you say something about Russia?"

"Do you not listen to anything I say?" Molly exclaims.

"That was my attempt at humor." I smile at her.

"You are hopeless." She shrugs.

"That's my middle name, baby." I strap on my smile and open up the door to the clicks and flashes of the camera."

"Colman! Colman! Over here! Colman! Over here, over here! Give us that smile, big guy! Colman!"

The cacophony of screams assaults me the second one foot is out the door. My smile grows.

Three Siv girls in the front row faint while two more Siv girls, who look about my age, pull up their shirts. There are a few adult Sivs, who I assume were brought along by their daughters or sons. They do not look happy to be here at all. Much to the dismay of Molly and the camera crews, I stroll over to the fence and notice that there is one girl in the back with her back turned to me. That never happens. People risk their lives to catch a glimpse of me and this girl is not turned in the right direction. Maybe she is blind? Yep, that's surely it.

The screaming is indecipherable pandemonium now. I reach the fence and Sivs frantically jab their arms through the chain-links wanting to touch me. Papers are shoved at me. There's something all of a sudden violent about it. Damn, that blind girl should have turned by now. I finish signing autographs, fill my pockets with all the numbers that are thrown on me, and kiss a Siv girl through the fence. Time to leave.

"Thank you for all being here. I have the best fans in the world. Thank you for making me the Alpha I am today! I appreciate you all."

I turn away and start heading back to address the reporters who are waiting for me.

"Colman! How are you feeling today? Is today your Execution? We would all miss you! Colman! How was your Encounter this morning? Were you hurt? When are we going to see the next Execution?"

Generally, towards the ends of these questions, the reporters lose their inhibitions and start foaming at the mouth, wanting to know the smallest details about me even though they can see everything already. I chuckle and give them a big smile and call on one of my camera crew.

"Yes, Vanessa."

"Colman, I was with you this morning when those two men attacked you at your apartment building. What crossed your mind that made you able to Execute them? I imagine you were not fully awake yet."

"Vanessa, great question," I say, as I hear a sigh escape from all the others standing there. "You know, I was thinking there is no way that I am going to let these two buffoons take me out there. I live in that building for Spike's sake. My Execution was not going to be in my only place of refuge. I also had a great breakfast this morning, so I was ready to go..."

"What did you have?" she interrupts.

"I had ten egg whites, scrambled with spinach, ham, and Mozzarella cheese. Then I had a bagel with salmon cream cheese. After that, I made myself a smoothie with spirulina, kale, egg yolks, bananas, strawberries, some coconut milk, protein powder, and apple juice."

The reporters love when I describe what I eat. Food is still limited in the Country and many Sivs don't even have enough to eat.

"Do you think you will have another Encounter today?"

"Yes, thank you, Vanessa, great follow-up question. First, I have to say that I know my team so well that I would know if someone was on my jet who was not supposed to be there. My private cabin is designed to keep me safe."

"Is there a second thing?"

"What?" I say.

"You said, 'First I have to say…'" she repeats, "so I wanted to know if there was a second thing."

"Oh yes there was a second thing. You look lovely today."

With this, the conclave of reporters turns on Vanessa and start snapping pictures.

Seconds later, my EYE shows me a news report saying that sources have confirmed that Colman Cai is sleeping with one of his own reporters. I silence the reporters' immediate slew of questions and then reject the rumors that were made four seconds ago. The hands are back in the air, waving back and forth, waiting to get picked. I go through this process for another seven minutes and then call for the final question.

"Colman. Rumors are circulating that the men who attacked you this morning were sent from Russia. Is this true?"

I glance over at Molly, only to see her smirking.

"Great question. I cannot comment on these rumors seeing as I did not interact with these men for very long but what I can tell you is that if these men were from Russia, I'd have to ask Russia to step up their training program. However, I must thank them for a great warm-up."

My crowd goes wild.

"Thank you, everyone, I look forward to seeing you all when I get to my next destination. Cheers."

With that, my morning press briefing is over, and I am escorted up the steps of the jet and into my cabin. I give everyone a big wave and smile as I duck my head inside then bolt for a seat next to the windows. I require that my windows are washed each time before I board. I can observe so much of the world from behind the glass – they are a protection and a barrier from the outside world. My Escalades retreat from the taxiing area and head back toward the exit. My camera equipment is loaded into the cargo area and the rest of my security and camera team file into their section of the plane. Sivs live such a simple life.

As I look back to the tarmac, I see there is a pin-shaped object flying towards the cars from a distance. I watch in awe as it strikes the first car of the escort. It blows up just as it reaches the gate. I start laughing. How dumb are these people nowadays? I mean, they missed me by a mile. In the Pit, guns are not allowed, but RPGs are permitted because EYEs can detect them within a mile radius.

But I liked that driver. Well, I don't like anyone, actually, but he was good at what he did. It's too bad he had to get blown up.

The jet starts to move and soon the plane has turned completely around so I can no longer see the massive ball of fire that encapsulated my old car. I lean back into my leather seat, close my eyes, and fold my hands into my lap. The pilot tells me that the plane is ready for take-off. One moment I am sitting still and then with a little power, I am racing along the earth, lifting into the air - life is amazing. I thank the pilot and close my eyes again so I can get ready to seduce the queen's granddaughters. I hope Vassar's teeth are in better shape than they were last time and the queen has a flame-retardant wig.

CHAPTER 4

London is vastly different from New York. I want to live here one day, but of course, this is an impossibility. I will never be able to live where I want. I was owned by Khan from the day I was created and will be owned until the day I am Executed. If that day ever comes.

Two hours after departing Obama International, we touch down at Heathrow Airport. The Country purchased a jet that was created with rocket engines instead of regular plane engines – because they can. I did what Molly told me and posted four times while I was in the air. One was a picture of me smiling. One was a picture of my abs. One was a picture of me lying in my empty bed with the caption: 'I miss you.' This was not meant for anybody in particular but gets a rise out of the majority. The final picture was me looking out the window 30,000 feet in the air. These posts are nothing special, but I did what Molly asked. That is all I am required to do: Follow orders and give people a show.

The jet taxis to the private terminal and I see the red carpet rolled out from where the stairs will touch the ground. My security team emerges from the back of the plane and walks toward the front while the camera crew files behind them and immediately bolts for their equipment in the cargo hold. Molly departs next but she is talking to someone walking next to her. I zoom on my EYE but do not have clear enough resolution to determine who it is. I swear Molly came onto the plane completely alone. Before I can dwell on the irregularity any longer, the pilot unlocks the inner chamber and lowers the stairs. Time to smile.

The co-pilot is still in her chair and I ask if she is leaving now or is going to move the plane. She doesn't say anything. I move a little closer and ask again. Then I get a stirring deep inside. She is not moving. I turn around. The cabin is empty. I switch modes on my EYE, scanning for any detectable heat signatures. No one is going to ambush me from behind. I refocus my attention towards the co-pilot and still, she is not moving. I reach up to tap her on the shoulder.

As I do, she spins around and throws me against the wall. *Good Spike is she strong.* She flips me over and tries to pin me against the chair. How inconsiderate. I turn my EYE back off because I already know this is going to be too easy for me. I let her slam me against the chair two more times before I get to work.

"You think you're invincible? You're wrong. The Country is going to kill you," she seethes, a proud sneer on her face.

She reaches for what looks like a filed end of a spoon. *Are we in prison?* As she goes to slam me a third time, I grab her hand and snap her fingers all the way back. I hear the pop and click as they dislocate, then break. Her hand falls limp but she keeps coming at me. Props to her; I have done that to huge, burly men and they cry out. I grab my half-finished Manhattan and throw the remains in her face. She momentarily falters and wipes at her eyes, so I use the moment to grab my backpack, trying to retrieve one of my cool powders from my Execution gadgets, but too late, she has recovered. Grabbing one of my arms, she brings it against her knee like she is trying to snap a stick for firewood. *Come on, lady, who do you think I am?* I cry out in pretend pain and she looks at me in surprise. Of course she looks at me in surprise, she probably thinks there's hope for her.

She starts flailing as I grab her by the throat and bring her nearer to the exit. I am standing fully upright in my cabin, arm outstretched, dangling her above the ground. There is a gasp from outside and I see my security team standing below me, smiling. They are always smiling when I am hurting someone. The members of my SQUAD are hoisting their equipment while the one in charge barks orders for the best shot. They missed the beginning of an Encounter; their bosses are going to be on their asses for that mistake.

"What do you mean the Country is going to kill me?" I whisper to her as the crowd erupts below me. "In case you didn't know, they *adore* me."

"Khan is scared of you," she gasps. "You're too powerful, even for him."

I step out onto the first step, still holding the struggling co-pilot, and wave her around for everyone to see. My security team is beaming, my SQUAD is quiet and filming, Molly is clapping, and the person she was talking to is just standing there staring at me. I still cannot get a good look at its face. Bored now, I throw the co-pilot into the air before I catch her by her head and throw her against the side of the plane. She is Executed on impact. I feel her lighten as her last breath leaves her. I drop her to the ground.

Usually I feel amazing after a kill, but I can't get what the co-pilot said out of my head and it unsettles me. The Country would never kill me. I am their main attraction. Khan adores me.

Right?

My crowd has been going wild but that Being on the ground is still just staring at me. We make eye contact. Its eyes are a piercingly blue – almost mesmerizing.

Then the strangest thing happens. My EYE becomes fuzzy and then my whole world starts to spin. I try to recalibrate my EYE and shake my head but all I see are stars. Looking towards my security team, who has noticed that for the first time ever something's off with me, Rosen and Cassidy start to ascend the steps to steady me. But as quickly as it came, my EYE reboots and my vision returns to normal. Miraculously, my SQUAD has missed the entire moment of confusion –

thank Spike. What the heck just happened with my vision? *It's probably your EYE glitching.* I am not designed to have any glitches with any bodily function, much less the most important part of my body.

What if this is... no. I don't have a Pitfall. That would make me less Alpha.

I shrug it off. I'm fine.

A second later, I regain composure and slap a smile on my face as I continue descending towards everyone. SQUAD has refocused and the usual questions are thrown my way. They are all so excited that I Executed yet another person before even stepping foot on London soil. I answer none of the questions though and instead make straight for my caravan of cars. I cannot shake the feeling of that Being watching me or the co-pilot's words. She must have been truly deranged to say such a thing but looking in her eyes as she said it told me differently.

I keep smiling as I step into the Bentley and give everyone a wave.

What the heck just happened out there? What was that glitch? It felt like my heart constricted and I couldn't get enough air. That has never happened before. I need to find out who that person was next to Molly. Maybe my drink was poisoned?

Doesn't matter. I'm still an Alpha. I look down at my once-bruised knuckles from the fight with the co-pilot. Already healed.

Only an Alpha, the Top Dog, can heal that fast. Me.

The Siv co-pilot remains motionless next to the front wheel of the plane. The body is about to be moved so my jet can be stored for later. I crane my head to see if the mystery Being is anywhere in my field of vision.

[Profile Match: None.]

Weird. I bring my attention back into the car and observe the contents of the Welcome Package. In it, there is a diamond stud, a bag of chocolates, a gold chain, a pair of new shoes which I think are Tod's, and my vial of blood. These people have clearly not done their research. I have not worn an earring since I was fifteen. I hate chocolate. Gold is no longer a precious metal in the Country. I have already promised Testoni that I would wear their shoes while around London.

The only thing they got right was the vial of blood.

I must have burned at least half a vial during that last Encounter and about a quarter during the one this morning. I reach into the bag and take out the vial. I give it a shake so the plasma and red and white blood cells can mix, then take my syringe out of my Tumi backpack, press it into the vial and then pull the end outward. I see crimson color stretch from the needlepoint all the way through the syringe until it is filled.

This syringe is my lifeline.

Spikes are the only beings that require an everyday transfusion of blood. Supposedly, Sivs make this stuff on their own and are required to donate it to the Spike Program. I wonder what life would be like if I did not have to rely on the blood of others to continue surviving. It is symbolic that they give up part of their life to sustain mine, while I am paid to take theirs.

The needle is still resting in my hand, poised at a vein but something stops me. *What if it is poisoned?* I shake my head. I'm being paranoid. Molly would not have let this enter my car if it was not approved by at least three different Keepers. But for some reason holding someone else's Life in my hand takes on a different weight with me today. *Why?* I shake off the unfamiliar feeling and inject the blood into my quadriceps. I feel the physical euphoria half a second later. My body is already eating this up.

Relaxing my head against the rest, the car starts moving and I am transported back to my reality. My team spends so much time transporting me to and from my events that I don't know if I have spent more of this Life alone or in the company of others. Really, we are always alone – whether we want to believe it or not. This independence is refreshing but sometimes I wish I could do what I want, when I want it. The caravan files past the taxiing jet, past the co-pilot's body, and towards the exit of the tarmac. Luckily there are no incoming RPGs this time.

England has outlawed the use of Spikes in every way. Obviously, the Country will send some Encounters my way to make sure I receive views, but Molly warned me that the English Government imposed a Special Permit for anyone entering for an

Encounter. My head costs around five million pounds which brings me an incredible amount of relief. Maybe I will be able to relax. Who would pay so much? Molly hates this, she only cares about money. Though I don't know what she's worried about. In the last thirty days, I have had approximately sixty-four Encounters. I Executed one hundred and twenty-nine Sivs and have fought and Executed another four Beta Spikes.

I am thoroughly exhausted from the past thirty days and have not received an adequate mental break. It suddenly occurs to me that that would explain my reaction today on the jet. *Yes, that is what happened.* The only thing I have to think about now is how hard I am going to party and how long it will take for me to get into the princess's bed.

The cars fly past the gates of the tarmac and drive onto the road reserved for private flyers. I do not have to smile right now but I find myself looking at my reflection, a gleam in my Arctic sky eyes.

I'd say it was a thrill to be in London for the first time, but since excitement is an emotion I don't know, I can't quite understand it, even on my own face.

CHAPTER 5

We are speeding past the blurry outskirts of London. During the Attack of 2025, some of the biological and chemical weapons diffused their way into England and the economy took a significant plunge as people feared for their lives and shut themselves in their dwellings. Berkshire, Hampshire, Oxfordshire, Cambridgeshire, Shireshire, Shirenotshire, and Howmanyshires ... everything was decimated as a result of the chemical compounds. The Prime Minister and Queen declared a State of Emergency, but they were too late. That was the day the bombs dropped.

As I look out the window, the gaping wounds in the earth remind me how destructive the human race has become. All over are remains of the once-picturesque English countryside. There are no signs of life. The only thing that protrudes form the ground are the gravestones where family members buried their loved ones. The people with money bought monuments, some of them tower above the tree lines and some more modest ones are inlaid into the dirt. The signs of suffering and death, that I have been designed to enjoy, mark the barren surface. Death is attractive.

The grey London haze, which only got worse after the Attack, seems to swallow the stones and monuments. Even from the make-shift highway, I can see remnants of great statues that have since fallen. Like my own life, it reeks of nothing. When you are born into an existence of inflicting pain upon others, nothing fazes you anymore. I see the way my security teams look at each other and the way Molly looks at me: They view each other like there is some connection holding them together. It is a connection I can never understand.

When I was younger, I took a laser and waved it between these people to cut whatever connection was holding them. I thought this would sever the relationship and they wouldn't be so happy, but nothing ever happened to them. I tried to mimic their faces to see if I could look at people the way they do to each other but there is no way I could ever achieve that type of mastery. It is either superbly artificial or … real. [Observe. Replicate. Eyes: Locked. Mouth: Small Upward Tilt at Corners. Nostrils: Slight Flare. Pupils: Dilate. Eyelids: Lower. Corner Eyes: Lower. {Insert Emotion.} Error: No Identification.]

Each time I tried to mimic them, the results would be inconclusive. Although I can manipulate my facial muscles, when I ran the Diagnostic on the EYE, it stated that something was missing from the equation. I asked Molly about this, a year after I Entered, and she said there was something special to be said about someone who was not able to care. She told me, "Colman, even if you could complete this action you wouldn't want to. You are special because you will never have to experience the pain of someone disappearing. I will one day be gone and then you will find someone else just like me and it will mean nothing to you. But me? I will never be able to find another Being like you. You should be happy that you have the gift that allows you relief from this."

Maybe she's right but I can't help but think there is a hole in my life that will never be filled. I try to feel something other than adrenaline, excitement, and the pleasure that killing gives me, but nothing ever surfaces.

I watch the statues rise and fall with the contour of the land until we arrive at Buckingham Palace. Suddenly, out of the corner of my eye, I see an object moving quickly through the desolation in front of the tree line. Thinking that it is an incoming RPG, an automatic surge of adrenaline jolts my EYE to life. I analyze the incoming object but instead of seeing my Distance Meter decrease as we move it stays the same. Is this thing not coming at me? [Weapons Analysis: No Threat Detected.]

My jet was the only plane scheduled to land within a three-hour segment. No other cars are traveling along the same route. *What can be moving that fast?* I continue to peer out the window and zoom on my EYE. As the resolution adjusts itself and I become more immersed in the scene in front of me, my heart rate continues to rise. What is happening to me today? My field of vision has shrunk tremendously which is one of the first things I learned not to do when searching for a target.

When the resolution finally stabilizes, I see that there is a figure racing through the countryside. *That is impossible.* How can a Siv keep pace with a caravan of cars speeding at 75 miles per hour? And yet, there it is. I run a cross-diagnostic test on my EYE to include heat signatures, motion sensors, and blood regression tests but it comes back as a positive match for a … Spike?

[Diagnostic Test. Begin. Heat Signature: Subject registers at 99 degrees Fahrenheit.]

[Diagnostic Test. Begin. Motion Sensor: Active subject. Speed 76MPH. Moving SW.]

[Diagnostic Test. Begin. Blood Analysis: Subject. Alive. Blood Type. AB. Error. Inconclusive.]

[Diagnostic Test. Begin. Blood Analysis: Subject. Alive. Blood Type. B. Error. Inconclusive.]

[Diagnostic Test. Begin. Blood Analysis: Subject. Alive. Blood Type. A. Error. Inconclusive.]

[Diagnostic Test. Begin. Blood Analysis: Subject. Alive. Blood Type. O. Error. Inconclusive.]

[Diagnostic Test. Begin. Blood Analysis: Subject. Alive. Blood Type. ABO. Error. Inconclusive.]

[Diagnostic Test. Begin. Blood Analysis: Subject. Alive. Blood Type. B. Error. Inconclusive.]

[Diagnostic Test. Begin. Blood Analysis: Error. Failed Analysis. Recalibrate.]

Adrenaline courses through my body, so much so I lose my sense of being and send my fist through the window to get a better look. The driver starts to slow but I yell for him to keep driving. I have to keep up with this thing. The driver speeds back up as I hear voices crackling through the car's intercom. The drivers behind me speed up while the crackling turns into screeching. I zoom out and poke my head through the broken window to have a better view of the scene. My security team and SQUAD are poking their heads out of the car – mirroring me. I know that I probably should respond to them, but I also don't want to lose track of whatever is tracking me. Activating the intercom was the worst choice I could have made. Molly is the loudest and most recognizable voice shrieking through the intercom.

"Colman, what the hell are you doing? We are not supposed to be speeding anywhere much less in a foreign State! The Country is going to be fined for this! Get your head back inside that damn car or you will not like the Being you have to face when we reach the palace!"

"Who is that racing alongside us, Molly?" I yell.

"What…" I hear her mutter. "Someone get me a visual … on the east and west side of these cars. Now!"

At that, cameras rotate to the decimated countryside, on either side of the car, as my SQUAD focuses on the woods – attempting to capture movement alongside the caravan. The heat-seeking setting is activated, and everyone is frantically scrambling to get a shot. Meanwhile, the cars are pushing 90MPH. I zoom in and look back towards the figure. It … it is a girl, her arms and legs pumping in a blur. She is still there. Turning towards the cars behind me, I am about to yell to Molly, confirming identification of the target, but she cuts me off.

"Colman, tell your driver to stop. We need to have a little chat," Molly says frantically as she cuts back on the intercom.

"What? If I lose pace of this girl, then I'll never be able to find her again. She's too fast."

"Colman! Stop the car now!" she screams.

I zoom all the way out now because the two cars, carrying my security detail, speed up to overcome mine. We are barricaded in and the only way to get out of it is if the driver rear ends the SQUAD car. My driver slows down then comes to a complete stop. Intensely fixated on the girl, I watch her as she continues running then disappears out of view. The cars are now nestled on the side of the bomb-riddled road as a pair of high heels and four pairs of Country boots approach my car. I am forcefully yanked out of the car. My security team saves Spike-mishandling for very rare occasions when they are angry. I know I've messed up. Molly pulls me in close and looks me straight in the eyes. Her hand is balling the front of my Henley, but I am six inches taller than she is – even when she's wearing high heels – so she has to shout at me to make up for the height difference.

"This is not what we had planned for this ride young Spike! How dare you not listen to me when I

[43]

speak to you? Do you even know how much trouble I am going to be in? You blazed past us and all I see are shards of glass flying back at my face. How did that happen? Did you throw them at me? Did something break? I have no idea how you can be this reckless on a ride through a State which has offered to host us!"

I open my mouth to speak but my smile is already too wide. What a weird reaction. I will never get over it, she gets so passionate so quickly. *What is it like to feel something like that?*

She continues, "How am I supposed to explain this damage to the Producers and Keepers monitoring you at home? You used an entire vial of blood just in your efforts to adjust your EYE back and forth, back and forth, back and forth, to run all those tests! Why were you even running them to begin with? There was no Being out there! I ran the same tests, and would you like to know what I came up with? Nothing! There was nothing out there. What were you doing? On top of all this, we have been cruising along at this speed for over twenty minutes. What do you think that will do to the agenda…"

Now this throws me. There's no way I was chasing her for twenty minutes. *No way.*

"What do you mean?" I say.

"I mean that at 11:02 AM I saw pieces of glass fly at me as you accelerated to one hundred million miles an hour and now, we are standing here at 11:24 AM watching you smirk at me while I scream!"

"That is not possible," I counter.

[44]

"Well it is possible, and if you do not believe me then go check the energy levels for your EYE. You just used it for, let me see here … twenty-one minutes and sixteen seconds."

She is right. My EYE's history says that same thing. What is going on?

"This is not going to be how this trip goes. I thought you would be grateful that I got you out of the Country so you can relax. Now you repay me by throwing pieces of glass in my face and telling me that some women are so obsessed with you that they have the capacity to run alongside your car just to see you?"

"I didn't say that," I say.

"You didn't have to. I know how you think." She takes a deep breath. "Look, our agenda was to arrive at Buckingham at 12:05 PM because the queen's granddaughters will not be able to greet you any earlier. You screwed it all up. It will probably be easiest to sit here and watch the grass grow for the next eleven minutes 'til we get back on schedule."

"I am fine with that," I say, seeing if I can rile her back up. She ignores me.

"In addition, I need to give you another vial of blood. You know what happens when you use the manual functions of your EYE. Next time please keep it on automatic. We have to carry all of our own blood supplies because it is illegal for English people to sell their blood for your use, you know that! If this happens again, I will not take it so easy on you and we will be back within Country borders before you can show your front teeth."

"Is that what you call easy?" I smirk.

She scoffs then retreats toward her car to pull out a reserve vial of blood.

I look around at my SQUAD and security detail. My SQUAD has all their cameras plastered in my face. I know they got that interaction on tape; they get everything on tape. I cannot see any of their faces but for once, they are silent and not asking any questions. There are many tricks that I have learned over the years but there is one constant - anytime I am made to look stupid, the footage is never aired. My Profile would take a hit if the world saw Molly screaming at me.

I have no clue what just happened, but I know for a fact I saw a girl. *I did not make it up.* My Diagnostic Tests may not have been saved in my History, but I know what I saw – no one can tell me anything different.

Molly stomps back and thrusts a syringe of blood straight into my neck. Before she removes the needle, I already feel more myself.

Our little roadside stop wasted seven out of those "off-agenda" minutes so after waiting another four minutes, I hop back in my car and tell the driver to move. I apologize to him, not because I feel bad but because Molly has told me I should.

He smiles at me and, in a wonderful British accent, says, "Sir, it is my pleasure. I am sorry that you had to go through that. Your female handler looks like she can handle about anything."

"She sure can," I say,

"Oh, and by the way, sir, I did catch a glimpse of that young woman."

I snap my head towards the driver's mirror so I am able to see his eyes. The driver is telling the truth and his intentions are sincere. He apologizes for speaking out of turn, but I thank him as he puts the car into drive.

I am not losing it after all. But why would Molly lie?

CHAPTER 6

At precisely 12:05 PM, the caravan pulls into Buckingham Palace for a royal greeting. Molly is incredible. Our entrance included a procession of the Queen's Guard in their uniforms and a smattering of Press from all around the world. Before 2025, the Queen's Guard wore huge fur hats, called bearskins, and red coats. They looked stupid. However, when the world Powers were attacked – the same day the missiles launched – a small band of specially trained insurgents tried to infiltrate each State's government - in the Country it was this place called the White House, in Paris the band destroyed the Eiffel Tower, in Russia it was the Kremlin and in England it was Buckingham Palace. The Queen's Guard had never come up against a threat such as this and every last one of them was killed, making it easy for the insurgents to slip into the palace. Now the Queen's Guard is among the fiercest warriors in the world and their uniforms portray that. They wear an all-black outfit with a black helmet, and no one can see their eyes underneath industrial strength sunglasses. They mean business, and now, they look it.

The Queen's Guard checks each of the cars in the procession before we are allowed in. There is a lot of 'hoorah, God save England' as the cars slip past the metal gates. Once we are allowed through, I see what I had come for. Like a creep, I zoom on their incredibly attractive faces.

And then there's the queen.

The years of war since 2025 had not been kind to the royal family. Quite a lot of the succession had been killed off in the years after the attack. The old hag, who had once been something like 20th in line, had profited from the war and unexpectedly inherited the throne, and she jealously guarded her prize. She is standing in front of her smoking hot granddaughters, blocking the view. I know for a fact that Vassar is attracted to me, but I wonder what Marist thinks.

Marist and Vassar are two of the most sought-after women on the entire globe and even though Vassar reeks of genetic engineering, the Sivs seem to like it. Genetic engineering is taboo across the world and consists of Spike Program-like techniques to alter embryos in the womb. Every State secretly partakes in it, and the queen's granddaughters are certainly no exception. States do not want to admit their association with the Pit, but egotistical, power-hungry bureaucrats will never forgo a chance to have offspring that exemplify the most desired qualities on the globe.

Marist is the younger one and is around my age – twenty or twenty-one. She has brown hair that falls to her shoulders and the most electric blue eyes that make Beings shiver. She is probably 5' 9" or 5'10" and would look exceptional as my side piece. She is slim – but not overly slim – to imply any type of malnourishment. She is the athletic type of fit, *just how I like them*. The last time I saw her, she was furiously punching me after I "accidentally" caught her grandmother's hair on fire. (All I wanted was to see if her wig was real or if that too was genetically engineered.) I can still remember her bright blue eyes widening in angry exhilaration as she fixated on what I had done.

Scanning her brings a rush of ... *something* to my chest. Not exactly the pleasure I get from killing, but a similar feeling ... my adrenaline begins to spike, like I'm getting ready to go on the hunt. *What?* The way she stands regally next to her grandmother, slightly annoyed that she has to be here, is edgy and enticing. The only thing awry is a small tear in her dress. No one else would notice these small details but I see everything.

Vassar, on the other hand, is probably twenty-four but – when she is not drinking – acts like she is ninety-nine and on the verge of death. She is charming but has a royal droll about her when she speaks, almost like it is rehearsed (which is probably is). Listening to her is less exciting than staring at a blank wall. She is also a replica of her grandmother in the way she stands and presents herself to the rest of the world.

But behind closed doors, it's a different story. Although I am more attracted to Marist, I have never spent a night with her. Vassar on the other hand... I recall to mind the details of that misbegotten evening. My time with Vassar was like being thrown through a meat grinder. I came out of her bedchamber with bite marks, scratches, and pieces of my hair missing. It was one of those nights that most people only dream about and I'm hoping that I get an encore. Though maybe with Marist this time...

The absence of a window makes it hard for me to gaze upon the three women inconsequentially so the queen and her granddaughters size me up from the royal steps as I do the same to them. I thank the driver for his service and, without waiting for Molly, who will not throw another temper tantrum in front of royalty, I swing open my door as a smile automatically adorns my face. I look back towards my SQUAD who are taking their sweet old time to get their equipment out. They are completely unaware that I am out of the car. The people crowded against the fence of Buckingham Palace are my audience and the noise that erupts when they see me is deafening. That must bother the queen's hearing implants. The British press core is also waiting for me, to the left of the queen's podium, so at least I have someone taping me. *Go for it.*

As I turn my back to the audience, to face the queen and her granddaughters, I crisscross my arms and grab the bottom of my Henley. Marist instantly recognizes what I am about to do, and she rolls her eyes in feigned disgust. *I like a challenge; don't you know that?* In slow motion, I see Molly emerge from her car and she looks towards me, her eyes instantly widening because she has seen this move more times than she can count. She could kill an animal with a stare like that.

Her eyes turn into slits and she mouths, "Don't you dare." *Oops, too late.*

I pull my top across my chest then up and over my head and the crowd unleashes the lust which has been swirling in their chests since I arrived. My camera crew is actively struggling to get their equipment onto their shoulders because if they miss the royal introduction, they are going to get reamed out by the Keepers. On the other side of the pedestal, the British press surges forward to get a better shot but I block them as I turn my body to square up to Her Royal Majesty.

Once it is off, I fling it over my shoulder. Behind me, the palace Gates creak as men and women alike press against the bars to get a better look. I reach down and undo my shoes, stringing them together and letting them hang off my shoulder. Marist is looking at me with absolute disgust. I am trained to see that reaction because in the Country if you look at a Spike with disgust, it shows a deviant behavior. The punishment for deviancy of any kind is Execution.

But seeing as how she's the queen's daughter, I'll let it slide.

Vassar licks her lips. Marist's eyes suddenly light up as she bursts into laughter. *Wow, she looks so much more attractive like that.* With the shoes and shirt off, I take my first step forwards. The wails of lust behind me are deafening but all I can focus on is how much I want Marist. The sunlight is shining from behind her and she has not broken eye contact with me the entire time. My smile turns into a smirk and I take the steps toward the queen and the granddaughters in stride.

The queen is a little old woman but is incredibly intimidating. Typically, she wouldn't offer her hand to the bastard of an illegal killing program but today she looks as if she wants to assert her dominance. *Bring it on, Queeny.* She defiantly places her wrinkly old hand in front of me. As is custom, I take her hand in mine and bring it gently to my lips. See, I have done this enough time to realize what happens next. I was engineered so that any physical connection is designed to be a one of a kind experience.

My lips come closer and her face drops as they press into her ancient skin. She senses that something is off and tries to pull away from me but, like I said, I am only doing what tradition dictates. As I place my lips on her knuckles, her pupils dilate and her head arches slightly as she closes her eyes. It takes five seconds for pry them back open and I see an absolute peace when she looks at me again. This time she smiles. I bow to her and face her granddaughters. I turn all my attention to Vassar, as she is the eldest. She looks at me like I look at a target during an Encounter; it is completely carnal. Vassar extends her hand, hoping that she can share the same experience her grandmother just had, but I do not want to embarrass her on television, so I just bow slightly.

"Vassar, it is my pleasure to see you again after so many years. Thank you for having me at your home."

"Oh, do shut up," she snaps. "My sister and I are still mad at you for the incident last time. How do you have the audacity to blow-torch a woman's hair, much less the Queen of England?"

God, she has not changed. I mutter a half-hearted apology and turn my attention to Marist because she is a marvel. If I did not know better, I would assume she was a Spike, or some other miracle of underground genetic engineering meant only for the wealthy. I lose my words in her eyes. They gleam like…like…like my own? There is an overly aggressive push from Molly behind me which thankfully snaps me out of this trance.

"Marist, hi."

"Is that it?" she hisses.

"What do you mean?"

"You gave my older sister a distorted apology and I get two words?"

"Uh, no. I am sorry, Princess. Ah, crap, that was not it either. Uhhhh…" I stutter, hearing gentle murmurs from members of my SQUAD. I am never tongue-tied. This will not look good on live TV.

"Colman, there are so many things you could say. Do you mean to congratulate me on the recent work I am doing to help England's poor? Or were you going to suggest that you would be honored to help me with my charity work during your time here? Or were

[54]

you going to apologize to me for our last meeting? Or were you going to say that it is your pleasure to be here, and you are grateful for our hospitality? Honestly, you have your pick of many things."

"Actually," I say as I recover my charm, "I was going to say, before you interrupted me, that you look stunning today and if you have the time, I would enjoy seeing the palace Gardens with you during my stay here. I will also be helping you on your endeavors with England's poor. It is quantifiably good work."

Marist curtsies to me and sarcastically mentions that it would be her honor, then leaves to go inside. I watch her walk into the shadows when Vassar slaps me across the face without a single word and puffs back into the palace following in her sister's wake. A gasp escapes from everyone around me. *I am digging this crazy today.* I now have a circle of cameramen and women around me, with the respective reporters stuttering about what they just saw.

The headline, "Jealous Vassar slaps the Country's Alpha" appears on my EYE. I do not know what jealousy really is. I read up on it but it seems highly illogical. You feel possession over someone and do not like it when other people feel any emotion towards that Being? Isn't every Siv allowed to feel attracted to me? That is my purpose in their lives, after all.

Molly wedges herself between the queen and me. I am still standing shirtless and shoeless on the steps of Buckingham Palace with five thousand people screaming my name behind me. I liked the feeling of being slapped in the face because I was able to take a break from smiling for once but something else has happened. I feel like I am floating outside of my own body. I see myself standing there looking at Marist as she retreats into the palace. I see my eyes stare in amazement as she does so.

I am not designed to feel anything in the 'normal' way, but right now I have this weird sensation where my heart inflates a little bit. I see it in my chest. What is happening to me? My vial of blood must have been impure this morning. First, I see some random girl running at 80 MPH and now I am floating outside my body and am seeing my heart increase in size? Molly pulls my arm and I realise everyone is looking at me like they are expecting me to say something.

"What?" I say.

"Did you not hear what the queen just said to you?" asks Molly.

"No, I am sorry, ma'am," I say addressing the queen. "I think I am a bit shaken after your granddaughter hit me."

"Mr. Cai, I apologize for my granddaughter's behavior. That was incredibly rude and no way anyone of our standing should greet any type of guest, no matter who they are. Please accept my apologies on her behalf. Will there be any way to cut that part out of the tape? It will cause a publicity nightmare for Vassar."

"I am sorry, but these cameras are live, as arranged by the Country. There is nothing I can do," Molly apologizes.

"Then I must go clean this up myself, please excuse me. Your quarters are in the south wing of the palace. The staff has been awaiting your arrival for quite a long time as they are huge fans of your performance ... as am I. Excuse me."

The queen winks at me as she excuses herself and that alone could function as the whole reason for my trip. Fanto and Rosen are pulling harder on my arms and I let them take me. They both know that they have no control over me, but I think their ears are hurting from the screaming. They initiate their Phase I EYEs so the rest of the team can track my location.

Molly comes running up to me when once the palace doors close. "Colman. I will not have this one bit. I told you that we are here to *visit* the Royal family, not to upset the royal family. We are not off to a good start and if you think ..."

"Have you even checked my ratings yet?" I ask innocently.

"No ... but ... no, I haven't. There is no need. I know how Sivs react to this sort of thing. They are protective of their royal family and you just insulted them ..."

"Molly, do me a favor and check my ratings." I have already seen the increase in approval ratings on my EYE, but this will help reaffirm that I am her boss.

"Fine, you know what ... see, look ... wait. How is that possible?"

"I need you to remember that although you are the best producer out there, that's in a large part because of me. I have access to more information than you do. You are simply my handler and travel agent. I know what works. You need to remember that my Profile is seen on a global scale. Although I may have taken a dip in England, Sivs in other States enjoy the fact that a Princess slapped me," I say, slipping my shirt back on.

"Let me set something straight for you ..." Molly starts.

I start to manipulate my face so that it looks like I am feeling guilt. [Replicate: Guilt. Eyes. Downturn. Mouth. Small Downward Tilt at Corners. Nostrils. Shrink. Pupils. Dilate. Eyelids. Lower. Corner Eyes. Lower. Lips. Quiver. Forehead. Flatten.]

Molly shrugs. "Ugh, never mind. You know what I want from this trip. Make sure it happens. If anyone needs me, I am going to be in my room. I need a break. Rosen, Fanto make sure he does not leave your sight."

"Yes, ma'am," they say in unison.

"Colman, you have three hours of free time until we have our first outing for Club Siv. The rules are as follows. Number one: do not leave this building. Number two: do not leave the sight of your security team. Number three: I know you are not going to follow number two, so you have to keep a tracking device in your forearm."

Out of nowhere, one of my SQUAD springs out of the crowd surrounding me and shoves a sharp, blinking pod under the skin of my inner arm. I stare in mild surprise.

"Am I supposed to say 'Ow'?" I ask condescendingly.

"No, that was for my enjoyment. Let me finish my rules. Number four: the princesses are off limits! We have already signed waivers with the Royal Family, as they do not want any of their members filmed naked and broadcasted around the world."

"I am certain they wouldn't mind if they experience it firsthand."

"I am not done! You already made a mistake sleeping with Vassar last time and we spent almost two million dollars bargaining with the Keepers to take that segment out of your tape. It is not going to happen again. Number five: if you do not obey numbers one through four then we are pulling you out of this State and are having the jet take you back to Country."

"One last question, Molly."

"Yes?"

"Will I be able to bring someone home from the club tonight if I am not allowed to sleep with the princesses?" I say sarcastically.

"Was that anywhere in my rules?"

"No. So does that mean I can--"

"You. Need. To. Behave. I hope I made myself clear."

"Crystal."

"Great. See you in three hours. Stylists are going to be over here to outfit you. I have to go tend to a few things," she says, sadly nodding at my security detail and walking away.

"Are you guys ready to have some fun then, eh, eh?" I say jokingly, looking at them.

Rosen and Fanto stare at me stoically before violently injecting a vial into my neck. The world fades from view but I recognize this compound, it isn't the first time they have injected me with it.

"Fine, I see how we are going to play this then," I slur as my security drags me away from the palace entrance.

CHAPTER 7

"Molly? What are you still doing here?" I say just seconds later. *Didn't she walk away from me only moments ago?*

She ignores me.

Why are her eyes closed? She looks so sad.

"Molly?" I say, trying to take a step forward but my feet don't move. "Come on, cut the crap. Let me go." I am panicking, making no sense.

Then she looks at me and instead of looking into her eyes, I'm peering into pure white light.

With a sensation I suppose like relief, I realize what's happening. This is the side effect of the tranquilizer. These kinds of dreams happen to me whenever they use this strain.

"You don't know anything," she breathes.

"Very funny, Molly, or should I call you Colman? Wow, I cannot believe I am talking to myself."

"You. Don't. Know. Anything," she repeats.

"I know everything," I spit.

"He is coming."

"Who is coming? Seriously, Colman, snap out of it," I say to myself.

"He is coming," Molly says, turning from me as she is engulfed in light.

"Who?"

"Khan," a voice says. It is not Molly's voice.

CHAPTER 8

I was created ten years ago, after incubating for ten years prior, but my cognitive development is that of someone who is eighty years old. I have explored the world through prose, poetry, plays, pictures, music, art, and sex. I learned to play instruments two days after my Entrance Day, learned to read four hours afterward, then began to paint hours after that. In a world that has been destroyed, things like art and music are hard to come by and are reserved for the extremely wealthy like me. Supposedly, I do all these things proficiently, with a great deal of technical skill, but I do not have the genius or passion for any of it that some Sivs do. I guess you need emotion for that.

Do I like these things? I do not know. I think I like music and art, mostly because they are forbidden for the masses, and it's a status symbol to have access to them. But I've been told they make people feel things, and whenever I hear music or see a piece of art, I feel nothing. Just emptiness, as if I was hearing only silence or staring at a blank wall. So other than Executing Beings and partying, I really do not have a lot else to keep my attention during the day.

Peering around the inside of Buckingham Palace, I am bored by much of what I see. The tapestries

[63]

are a little faded but otherwise in immaculate condition, the paintings of past kings and queens have been restored, and even the marble busts and crystal chandeliers gleam of a lost time. But they are nothing to me; they neither attract nor repulse.

There is a concept called beauty – which I researched after a Keeper explained it to me. Beauty is a feeling when you combine physical attractiveness and emotional love for an object. He explained to me that when something is 'beautiful' it captures your attention and holds it – making you wonder about its origins and its qualities but most of all about what will happen to it in the future. You never want to see it disappear. The Keepers said that I will never be able to experience a Being as 'beautiful' because I am set on destroying and conquering them.

The gardens outside the palace will die when cold weather comes. The marble busts will begin to crack and crumble. The paintings will chip and fade even more. The crystals will one day fall out of their holdings and will turn to dust. The only thing I can imagine being beautiful is music because music can live forever. Music is outlawed in the Country but the wealthy, and people from other States, still have access to it. We are subjected to pre-2025 sounds or music from other places because musicians from the Country are Executed if found.

After the first thirty minutes of wandering through the grand hallways – feigning interest as I look at portraits of the ancient royal family members –

security and SQUAD are noticeably bored and off their game. With no need to be on the lookout for Encounters, they are practically glorified baby-sitters. I try talking to them, but they do not reciprocate. Nevertheless, I researched Buckingham Palace before we came and noticed that the building plan had "undisclosed passageways" littering the drawing. I was determined to find one and snake my way through the underbelly of the beast. Plus, it would help get rid of my overbearing security detail.

Approaching hour two, I committed to finding a passageway after catching a glimpse of a long white dress disappearing around the hallway. I thought to chase after it but imagined that if it were the queen, she would try to seduce me after the way I made her feel this morning. *Molly never said anything about the queen, only the princesses...* Still, that is not something I would enjoy.

As hour three approaches, now frenetically using my EYE to locate a hidden entrance, I start to get more excited as I think about what the evening has in store. What mysteries does Club Siv contain? I doubt that the English can "throw down" like Sivs in the Country but I ought to give them a chance and not make any rash judgments.

I am about to give up and return to my room when I see a sliver of light coming from a crack in the wall. I stop and pretend to look at a tapestry as to not alert my baby-sitters – so I can get a better view of where the light is coming from. I turn on my EYE and as it scans, "Passageway" returns in the suggested conclusions. I turn slowly, so as not to raise suspicion; my SQUAD turned off their cameras moments ago and all four security cameras are glazed over. Using my EYE to gain access to the automated lighting in the palace, I override the firewalls and shut off all the lights. Yells erupt from my SQUAD but unfortunately, my security is back on full alert. I have twelve seconds to open this door and bolt into the passageway before my EYE is blocked from the system.

I immensely enjoy it when this type of thing happens.

T-minus eight seconds: I run my fingers all over the passageway entrance to find the handle to open it. T-minus six seconds: Fanto and Rosen are calling out my name and my smile gets bigger. They honestly should have seen this coming. T-minus four seconds: my hands fumble for a brief moment then slide into a wooden panel just above waist level. I push it and it clicks. The door opens and beams of light come streaming out. Cassidy and Downey locate me as they sprint toward the open door. T-minus two seconds: I jump through the passageway and slam the door shut. T-minus one second: luckily, I hear the door click and know it is locked.

Realistically, my security is not going to stop until they find me, but I estimate that it will take them at least a few minutes to get the door open. The banging on the door gets louder as Fanto and Rosen join Cassidy and Downey. *It is not my fault if they cannot do their job*. Strolling down the empty inner corridor, I come to a fork and, although I highly doubt that people are waiting to ambush me, the years in the Pit has made me exceedingly careful. [Initiate: Heat Seeking. Clear.]

I take the right passageway and keep following that until I reach another wooden door. Smiling to myself, adrenaline rushing and bubbling inside, I am about to open it when voices sound from within. *Princess Vassar and Princess Marist?* Not only am I already super awesome, attractive, smart, and funny but I am so lucky as well.

"Marist, if you screw this up for me, I will never talk to you again. He was mine to begin with," Vassar says, and I already like where this is going.

"Vassar, how many times do I have to tell you that I am not interested?"

Oh. I do not like where this is going…

"Yes, you do! Just admit it. You like him and want to sleep with him."

"That is so far from the truth! How can you even say that? Your obsession with sex is so unhealthy – not everyone's sole purpose in life is to sleep with someone else."

"I saw the way you looked at him."

"Vass, that's how we were both taught to look at guests, or do you not remember?"

"But the way you looked at him was different."

"You sound like a whiny little toddler."

"I do not!"

"Yes, you do." She switches tones to imitate her sister. "'Oh Marist, stay away from him so I can have one night alone with him. He is going to rescue me from the tower I am locked in and make me happy beyond my wildest dreams.' Listen to yourself! You sound ridiculous!"

"He *is* going to make me happy beyond my wildest dreams! You do not know because you are still a child."

"Excuse me?"

"You heard me."

"This conversation is over. I do not have the time nor the energy to entertain you when it comes to that Spike. Go sleep with him if you must! However, you should remember what happened last time."

"Yeah I gave him the best time of his life."

3% true, 97% untrue.

"Well, I am not going to defend you when grandmother has to clean up your mess."

"The only mess will be in the bedroom and I can assure you grandmother will not be going in there."

"You are so disgusting! Listen to yourself. Is this the type of thing that actually takes place in your mind?"

"No, it happens in real life."

An exasperated sigh. "I am done. You win. Get yourself ready, we have to get changed and fitted for Club Siv tonight. That animal – that pig – made us agree to look "more Country" when we accompany him – ridiculous."

Who did she call an animal? Is that me? That cannot possibly be me? I am not pink, nor do I have a curly tail, and I do not roll around in the mud and get dirty. *Actually, I take that last part back.* Fortunately for me, my thoughts are interrupted because the original passageway door splinters as a large echo seeps through the hallway. I sprint back towards the entrance in just enough time to be out of sight when the princesses open their door. My security comes shouting all sorts of ridiculous orders. I begin to lower my shoulder - it's time to go bowling.

I see them from a distance and then make eye contact with Rosen who is in the lead. He sees me coming and panic washes over his face. He knows what happens when I lower my shoulder. He stops then begins to retreat but it is too late for them. My muscular upper body is engaged, and I barrel through them with a perfect strike. Everyone except myself is on the ground and they are panting and moaning as they begin to regain their balance. They greet me with no emotion, partially because they all knew this was going to happen at least once and partly because I know they are glad to have some action in this boring day.

"Colman come on. We have to meet Molly in your room so you can get dressed for tonight," Rosen says.

"Ah, so King Pin can still speak. That is wonderful news to hear," I say sarcastically.

I can tell that the rest of the team finds this humorous but, for some strange reason, Rosen does not like it. I take his fist to my face, landing against the wall from his punch. I appreciate the audacity of these people and as I prepare to retaliate, Downey catches my hand mid-air and transfers my momentum, so my fist ends up puncturing the wall. My knuckles are slightly scratched but nothing a little pre-party blood transfusion won't fix. I apologize to Rosen and the rest of my team out of respect – like Molly taught me – which seems to calm them down.

"I want to thank you all for trying your very best. However, your best is still not good enough. I suggest that each one of you request a workout program from the Keepers. When you are in charge of the most Famous Alpha in the world, it is your duty to stay up with me. Now, where is my room?" I say with a smile.

Walking back towards the passageway entrance, the conversation between Marist and Vassar replays in my head. What possible reason could Marist have for not finding me attractive? I literally bowed to her - shoeless and shirtless - which usually is enough to make to make anybody wobble. I wonder if she has allergies. The seasons are changing here in England. Someone should really get her on some medication or give her a blood transfusion or something.

I find my room and when I open up the doors, I find Bella, armed with a brush, pomade, and makeup, standing next to the chair while Roberto is laying my clothes on my bed for this evening. This is a good sign. It means it's time to party.

CHAPTER 9

Tonight's outfit consists of black lace-up leather-cap Testoni loafers, black Cavalli jeans, and a dark purple vintage Versace button down. Bella and Roberto both run over to me and give me a huge hug when I enter the room.

"Colman! I heard that you got into some trouble today," Bella says in her incredible Jamaican accent.

"You of all people should know life is not as fun without a little trouble. Come on, now."

"Then it's time for you to look amazing for tonight!"

"You know what I am talking about, Bella. Roberto, it is so good to see you as well, my man."

"Sir, it is my pleasure to be here. Roberto was worried when he did not originally get the invite to come to England. Oh! Roberto was so worried. What would our knoflíček do without us? We are going to make you look amazing. Leave it to Roberto. Now sit, sit!"

With that, they pull me into the chair and order my team to undress me. They peel off my shirt, remove my shoes and socks, undo my Saint Laurent jeans, slip off my Calvin Klein underwear and then proceeded to wash off the dried blood and gel out of my hair. These two have been with me since my Entrance Day and have seen me naked in the flesh more times than any other Beings on the face of the globe.

Other people have seen me naked on my Profile so many times at this point that I am surprised there is still an attraction to me. *No, who am I kidding?* That does not surprise me at all! I read an old book called the Bible that there were these two Beings who got naked and then did not like being naked so they went and hid themselves. What? How could you not like being naked? I mean, going free is the best way to be. Well, especially when you look like I do.

I sit in the chair, scrolling through my EYE as Roberto shampoos my hair and Bella works on setting up my IV of blood. I am going to need to give a little more thought to how I should approach this Marist/Vassar situation. I do not want to pursue Vassar when it is obvious that she's obsessed with me. If she could tire me out the last time, I do not want to know what a super-charged princess can do to me this time. *Actually, I do want that...* Wait, no I do not. It might be too much and as if she's in my head, Molly aptly reminds me of the contract as I am thinking this.

Retrieving their individual Profiles, I scroll through the princesses, looking for something that can give me a better indication of who they are. Vassar's Profile reminds me of a snake from a children's story. This snake may look harmless, but this snake could also eat every one of the other characters in the story. All over her Profile there are subtle controversial messages, quotes from Spikes and Famous Sivs, and pictures from her Famous outings. It is relatively ordinary ... but isn't everybody's? I hesitate before retrieving Marist's. *Do I want to open up that can of worms?*

I pull her Profile up anyway because I can't resist. As I wait for my EYE to sift through Profiles, I see that the blood has started dripping from the IV and the two stylists are so focused that they do not see me looking at them. Bella has moved on to my makeup, Roberto has finished washing and drying my hair and now is applying the pomade to it.

"Roberto, remember it has to flip to the right."

"Who is the stylist here? You or I?"

"Just a reminder," I say.

"Thank you but I remember."

The clothes are laid out on my bed, each article an endorsement for a different designer. That outfit will probably earn me four million dollars by the end of the night, and I thank Khan for creating such an ingenious program. I hope the princesses are a little bit more receptive to the outfits my team had picked out for them. They may have called me a pig but that is before they see how much they need my help. A second later my EYE notifies me that Marist has been found and the files are decompressing.

Her profile is private and incredibly different from her older sister's. Strewn throughout the files are paintings of bodies, landscapes, architecture, and wildlife. Then there are pictures of England framed by verses of old-world poems. She must have taken these pictures somewhere deep in the countryside because there are no not remnants of war or a single silhouette of a building. I know the wonders of post-production, but I believe that these are natural. Poems from Keats, Shakespeare, Wordsworth, Tennyson, Shelley, Blake, Byron, Eliot, Milton, Kipling and so many more, scaffold the visuals. The first photo is of a frozen lake and underneath she scribed William Sharp's *A Crystal Forest* and added,

> *For in that earnest silence is perceived*
> *In the murmur of every sleeping being*
> *Come, gaze at me*
> *For so still I be.*

I look around at Bella and Roberto to see if they see this as well. *What a stupid thought, of course, they can't; it's embedded in my cornea for my own private viewing.* But after digesting this photo I know I do not have to dig through anymore to understand this girl. I recover as Molly bursts through the open doors of my room, a smile on her face.

"Colman inject the rest of the blood. The IV is going to take too long for what I have to tell you next! You are not going to believe who is going to be at Club Siv tonight!" she exclaims.

"Let me guess, is it perhaps Beacon Torin?"

"You are absolutely zero fun. How did you know that?"

"Molly, I see everything before you do! Look, I am willing to let you present my news to me, but you have to stop asking me how I know this. That is the definition of insanity, asking the same thing but expecting different results. This answer is not going to change, and this has been going on for ten years."

"Okay slow down there, champ, it is merely a question," she splutters. "Do you know what this means for us ... you?"

"No, that was a good question, bravo."

"It means that your ratings and Profile are going to skyrocket tonight! All Beacon has been talking about in the Press is about wanting to get with you and we can make that happen tonight! This is so exciting. So tonight, make sure you are looking good because we will get a bonus of two million dollars if ..."

"What if I do not want to sleep with her?" I ask nonchalantly.

"What? When has that ever been a problem before? You are going to get money and fame. If you play your cards right, you also might get some power ... her male Siv Donor, after all, is ..."

"Yes, yes, the Premier of Australia. I understand. What is she doing over here? Shouldn't she be hunting crocodiles or something?"

"Does it matter? I must go and make sure all the preparations are ready. Bella, Roberto, once Colman leaves, make sure this room is camera-ready and spotless for tonight's Encounter. Understand?"

"Yes, miss," they say.

"Wonderful! I am so excited! Colman, finish prepping because within the hour the Queen's Guard will be escorting you to Club Siv. Talk about a royal entrance, am I right?" she squeals as she leaves.

"Great," I mutter.

"Colman, you will have fun tonight. No matter what. No worry about Miss Beacon, yeah? You no be disrespectful."

"I know, but I wanted to enjoy my night out and have free time for once with no attachments," I grouse.

"Colman," Roberto interrupts, "no, no, no, no, no. Roberto is not going to have you complain about your good time and bad time. You live in a good time. No, no, no, no, Roberto will have this no longer. Sit back and let your two friends take care of you."

"What did you just say?" I say. I whip around and look at Roberto; neither of the stylists make eye contact while all the color in their faces drains away. They have seen death.

Sit back and let your two friends take care of you. I do not have friends. Who is he talking about? It is illegal for anyone to have a Spike as a friend, because that goes beyond mere affection and adulation.

"Nothing, sir," Roberto looks more confident as he regains composure and Bella does the same.

"Yes, you did, you just said, 'Sit back and let your two friends take care of you'. What does that mean?" I say evenly.

Roberto studies his fingernails. "Roberto never said that."

"Yes, you did. Just now. I just heard you say it. I can replay this conversation back on my EYE for you to hear."

"Sir, that is not a good idea."

"Why?"

"You will hear nothing."

"Yes, I will. I just heard you say it. My EYE listens and tapes my whole day. Listen." I open up the history in my EYE and look for our past conversation. I scroll all the way down but when I get to the clip from the last minute, I am faced with '=silence' between the times of 5:24:35 PM and 5:25:35 PM. That is strange. *I was just talking to them, wasn't I?*

"Sir, please, let us not stay on this silly mistake. Let Roberto and Bella dress you … yes, let us help Colman get ready," he says reassuringly.

"Ok, I apologize for that. I have felt very off today for some reason. I may have to go in for an overnight tune-up after my Encounter tonight."

"Yes, yes, no worry for you. Roberto is happy. Bella, are you happy to dress him?" Roberto chimes.

"That my job, Colman. Don't fret," she adds.

"Let me get dressed, I can help you set up the room for tonight and then you can escort me to the palace gates."

"Yes sir," they say in unison.

Fifty-five minutes later I am back surrounded by my SQUAD members, who are all dressed up. Security has tonight off as the Queen's Guard will be escorting me in and out of the club. SQUAD are all wearing matching Hugo Boss tuxes and black Testoni shoes. *Testoni is certainly getting their money's worth with product placement.* I seriously cannot believe that out of everything to survive post-2025, the thing that bounced back the quickest was fashion. Why couldn't it have been something more … useful?

I am right on schedule but where are the princesses? Damn, they better not be arguing about the clothes. The agreement was that I get to dress them if they have the privilege of going out with me. But no sooner am I done thinking that I hear the unmistakable click of high heels echoing from the granite hallway above.

My body unconsciously starts groaning for Marist and the Queen's Guard does not seem to hear me or want to pay attention to me, but my SQUAD just aired my reaction live all across the globe. But alas, the Louboutin shoes are attached to Vassar's body. She looks stunning and eye-sexes me which ultimately turns me off. A red Michael Kors dress sticks to her body with cutouts at her hip in a "V" section, and a slit that begins at her ankles and goes all the way up. The confidence Vassar displays is almost comparable to the amount I exhibit when I walk out of my apartment every day.

My rationale is that clothes should be a self-expression of your personality and should not necessarily flaunt how much money you have. So, when I walk out of 220 Central Park South, I look like the epitome of sex and violence. Vassar floats down the steps and stops right in front of me. She eye-sexes me again and gets right in my face, smiling as she leans to the left side of my face, whispering in my ear.

"I must commend you on your wardrobe choice. I insisted on wearing the La Perla dress you had sent but my instructions were clear. Red, anyway, is a color of passion. I look forward to having you take this off me tonight."

Vassar flounces away making sure that my stunned camera crew has some shots of her and her incredible body. I look back at her as she does so, and she winks and blows me a kiss.

No! Wrong move, Vassar!

My eyes widen and she instantly realizes what she just did. It is regular for Sivs to be attracted to me but the way she presented herself is an expression of care. *Care is forbidden.* Her security flocks her, also realizing what happened, forming a protective ring. It is one of the most punishable offenses to show any type of care for a Spike – especially on live broadcast.

With the Queen's Guard huddling around Vassar as they push her through the entrance, the sound of McQueen pumps strolling across the hallway redirects my attention. The main show, Marist, is coming. The clicking gets louder and one slender, yet muscular, leg appears around the banister.

From the shoes, my gaze traces the outline of the smooth skin … it surpasses my wildest dreams. Marist rounds the corner and one of the cameramen unsteadily drops the camera. The Queen's Guard seems to ignore the woman in front of them, but I cannot say the same for my SQUAD. They are not missing a single detail of her descent down these stairs. Marist is wearing a black La Perla dress made entirely from thread and crystals. You can see her skin underneath it and there is one long slit up her left leg to her hip.

Julia Haart made this dress before the Attack, for a celebrity by the name of Kendall Jenner for a Met Gala. I found it when I was at the La Perla fashion show last year in the vintage room. I am so glad Team Cai could procure this dress for this occasion. Marist continues her descent down the stairs, and she does not seem to notice any of the attention she is receiving. Her head is tilted upward, ignoring the world around her, and as she gets to the bottom of the stairs, I step forward to greet her. Yet, she does not break stride, taking a hard right towards the exit as her heel hits the floor – completely ignoring me.

That response does not compute.

Immediately, I want to be set on fire. Roll me in gasoline, throw me on a raft, light a match and watch me burn. The way my body is heating up, adrenaline rushing from the thrill of the hunt, tells me that I am already close to achieving that. *How does she have the audacity to ignore me?* The look on my face will be guaranteed to make the highlights tomorrow morning but I do not care. No Being is watching me now anyways. My EYE feels dry in my head and the cotton mouth has returned. I turn my gaze to follow her out the doors and everything except her silhouette goes black.

What am I thinking right now? She disappears behind the doors and my world comes crashing back down on me. She did not even stop to see me. That is so hot. She did not even look at me. That is so hot. She acted like no one else was in the palace. That is so hot. I want to be hot with her, someone get the matches. As the world comes spinning back at me, I am swarmed by the palace and Country reporters.

"Colman! Colman! Mr. Cai! Sir! Colman! Sir! What was that about? Are you and Princess Marist fighting? Did you pick out her dress? Did you know she was going to ignore your advance? Colman! Colman! Colman! How long has this feud been going on? Will Princess Marist receive any type of your royal treatment tonight for that action? Vassar or Marist, who wore it best? Colman! Sir! Are you going to talk to them tonight? Has a royal feud began?"

Still ruffled, but quickly resorting to normalcy, my autopilot kicks in.

"Ladies and gentlemen, enough questions. This entire night has been planned down to the last detail. Princess Marist is extremely focused on her appearance tonight and she did not want to be disturbed or distracted. In response to your questions…let me see. No. Yes. Yes. Not a feud. No. I cannot make that decision that is up to the viewers. Yes. No, I answered that already. Please, it is time for me to depart. Any remaining questions can be addressed to Molly at this time. Good night."

Molly steps up as the Queen's Guard pulls me away from the sea of reporters. I am so turned-on, itching to pin my quarry, that I feel bad for whoever the guard is in front of me. As she walks out the doors, the train of Marist's dress disappears into her car and I am left speechless as I get into my own. The two princesses are transported in the first car, Queen's Guard in the second, me in the third. I bend down to avoid hitting my head on the Bentley's roof and crash onto the seats. Good thing I had my transfusion this evening. Tonight is going to be one hell of an experience, and I have a feeling I'm going to need it.

CHAPTER 10

The day has taken forever but I am finally at my favorite part – the party. There is no other activity in this world where you can so totally free your body. And while I do genuinely respect all types of music, EDM, Indie, Alternative and House music are by far the greatest out there. There is a Power within each one of them that exudes youth, attraction, movement, nature, and the soul all at the same time.

As we approach Club Siv, I can already feel the energy flowing from each Being in this club. The lights welcome us as we pull into the half circle where are to be dropped off. At the beginning of each night, it is a requirement that myself and the company I am with are all photographed entering the club. Not only is the rest of the world able to see who I am wearing and who is accompanying me but, concerning liabilities, it is also better for my team to make it seem like each individual is entering and leaving the facility of their own accord – which they are.

Once my door is opened, I step out, simultaneously buttoning the Prada jacket I was given. Vassar is already out and probably has made her way through four or five drinks because security has to steady her as she steps out. Marist's door is not even opened so I make my way towards the entrance of the club to pass the time. Vassar greets me and a few hundred photographs are captured of just us two. I look over to Marist's door, but it is still not opened so I pull one of my guards close and ask them what is going on.

"Sir, the princess had a few technical difficulties with her evening wear, and she is taking the time in the car to fix this."

"Wonderful, thank you," I say.

As Sivs from all over the globe stream in around me, taking their own pictures and making their way into the club, I fixate on the thought of Marist. I am asked for an endless number of autographs and I oblige because it is better than irrationally having to worry about someone else. After waiting another four minutes and thirty-nine seconds, I make my way down to the car. I reach for the handle but by some stroke of luck, it opens and out steps Marist.

"I was getting worried that you wouldn't show," I smise.

"What can I say? You asked me to dress up in this ridiculous dress, come out to this over-extravagant club and then pose on your arm like I am your pet..."

"Marist, that is not my intention at..."

"So, I better at least make sure I am looking pretty bloody brilliant, right?" she says, cutting me off.

There is nothing for me to say. She pushes past me and gravitates toward her sister. I wait as they take their preliminary pictures and then someone pushes me forward to join them. Marist entrances me; the effortless air about her shimmers like glitter in sunlight – even though we are in the complete dark. She knows what angles to pose when the cameras flash, she appears physically aloof even though her eyes show how focused she is, and I realize that she does know the type of power she is wielding. She tilts, turns, and swirls for every single flash – not missing a beat. It is like watching the dance of a beautiful bird of prey.

She is so effortless that I forget where I am. Shapes shimmer and fold in on themselves around me, so much so, that I grab onto one of the Queen's Guard to steady me. They nod, and Vassar grabs my hand to walk in. I am greeted by the smell of overly applied cologne, perfume and sweat. The music is blaring through the speakers, the lights are flickering, alcohol is flowing, people are dancing in cages scattered throughout the club. I am smiling. I saunter past the bouncers who are staring in awe as one of my favorite songs plays through the speakers - "We are the Hearts" by EXGF. The lyrics and rhythm echo in my ears.

I had forgotten what it's like to be in a State where music isn't banned, like it is in the Country. It's intoxicating. The giant crowd is swaying, kissing, grinding, kissing, touching, kissing, to the melodies being broadcasted from huge speakers from every visible surface in the place. Sivs are wandering around offering drinks to others, dressed in their best clothes; there is exposed skin everywhere. In my euphoric state, I forget that I am responsible for a few more pictures with Marist and Vassar before the night gets away from

[85]

us. I turn around but before I make it to Marist, Vassar comes out of nowhere and grabs my crotch with her left hand holding another drink with her right.

"You got me right where you want me, Colman. Tell me what you are going to do with me."

"I am going to call your guards for you."

"No please don't! I will stop."

"Vassar, we have a contract together. My country signed a contract with your grandmother, the queen. Encounters are strictly off limits during my stay here. If I break it, I will lose more than a license to be here."

"Screw the queen. She has not had any action in like a million years."

I have to agree with her on that point.

"But it is still a contract and I am required to uphold that. I have to respectfully decline."

"Fine, whatever, screw you. You know how many men do want to have sex want with me?" she slurs again.

"Maybe you should lay off the drinks?"

"Screw you Colman!" she yells and walks away.

She heads toward the bar for another drink as a black swish disappears from view. *Marist, baby, here comes Colman.* I make my way through the crowd and catch a clear view of the back of Marist's head. Surging through the congested dance floor, fighting off a couple basically having sex there, I reach out and grab her arm.

She twists on me and rotates my arm violently, breaking the synovial hinge joint in the process.

Dammit. Give it twenty seconds and it will be able to repair itself.

"What the hell..." she starts.

"Marist, sorry, it's me. It's me!" I stutter.

"Colman, seriously, back off. I am not in the mood."

"Wait, come on, tonight is supposed to be fun."

"Yes, you have Beacon for your fun."

"You know as much as I do that I do not want that Encounter to happen."

"Oh yeah? And how do I know that?" she asks.

"Have you watched the replays? Did you see the way I looked at you today? Let me buy you one drink."

"Don't play this game with me. I know you can do anything with your face to mimic a real emotion. That was a rehearsed reaction. It was not authentic. You cannot feel anything except the pleasure that relates to conquering another Being. I will not be playing along in this little game. I am not an object solely to be used to make you feel good ... Colman, are you listening to me?"

The truth is I am not. I just made eye contact with Miss Australia herself – Beacon Torin. Dammit, I should have used the "Avoid" setting on my EYE, but it is too late now. She tips the bartender and brushes off the guy who's drooling over her before she sees me. Marist follows my gaze and snorts.

"Wow, that took you probably five seconds longer than I thought. Let go of me! I will take your stupid pictures; I will tell the Press that we had a great night, I will not, however, be your side piece in any capacity. I have business to do here anyway."

With that, she storms off towards the VIP section where a behemoth of a man escorts her behind a screen. Really, she will bang the bouncer but not even dance with me? *I should stop being respectful.* Already losing track of time, a whiny screech brings me back into the thick of things as Beacon crosses the dance floor, heading straight toward me.

Screw it. *If it is ratings Molly wants, it is ratings she will get.* My night is over anyway. A smile graces my face and Beings all over the club magically look towards me as I prepare the charm. My smile must give off a pheromone or something because before I know it, a direct walkway is cleared between Beacon and me.

"Beacon. How are you?" I say blandly as she approaches me.

"You know, Colman, my male Donor is teaching me how to take over his position as Premier of Australia. It is really quite a Powerful position…"

"Wow, I wouldn't imagine that running a country is hard work," I say sarcastically. She does not catch on.

"That's what I thought but, Colman … I am not necessarily here to talk. Do you get what I am saying?" she slurs.

Are these girls serious?

"Absolutely, babe. Let's dance."

"Ah…" Beacon begins to respond.

"But hey, let's not talk, let's keep this physical."

She gives me an overly awkward wink and pushes herself towards my chest, balling her hands in my shirt. She draws a big breath like she is gasping for air and attaches her mouth to mine. I do admit, although I am not physically attracted to Beacon per se, there is something about a woman who goes after what she wants. Especially one I haven't had yet.

I close my eyes and try to imagine that it is Marist because that would make this whole situation so much better. My SQUAD must be close because I am alerted to the gentle notification in my EYE showing the live news article, "Money, Fame, AND Power? Cai is a Triple Threat." Molly must be happy. My SQUAD must be happy. My Keepers must be happy. I only feel the physical closeness and Beacon's breath on my neck. Is that happiness? If not, then am I lacking happiness? What is the opposite of happiness?

Beacon and I dance the rest of the night. Vassar sees us together and punches me right in the crotch. That will take a little longer than twenty seconds to heal but still no pain. Molly chimes in around 2:15 AM, alerting me that Vassar has left the club and is heading back to the palace. *Give me fifteen more minutes and then I will take the future PM back.*

"You just made us two million dollars. We can celebrate tomorrow. Put on a show. I will talk to you tomorrow," Molly messages and signs off from her Communication software.

It is up to me now. At 2:30 AM, I manage to pry Beacon off me and ask her to come back to the palace. She is what the Keepers call "overjoyed." This is physical and mental euphoria above the normal and average level of happiness. She grabs my hand and we maneuver through the crowded club towards the entrance. Remembering Marist, having not seen her all night, puts me on edge. She disappeared over four hours ago. I tell Beacon to wait near the door as I locate Marist. [Location: Marist Khair Aston. Initiate. Location: The Globe. Stop Tracking.]

The Globe? When did she leave to go there and more importantly, what is she doing there? I want to ignore the thought, but something is wrong; I can feel it. Walking back towards Beacon, I try to phrase how I will break the news to her. It will be two million dollars lost but there is something about Marist that makes that worth it.

"Beacon, look, I am really sorry but…" I begin to say, taking two steps in her direction.

She heaves forward, clutching her stomach, as I near her. *Good Spike, I hate vomit.* If she is throwing up, she may very well have done my job for me. I don't take home drunk women.

But as I survey the scene, I realize that nothing came out of her mouth. As she stands up, a red stain appears in the front of her dress; that redness starts to diffuse to the other parts of the fabric. She is dripping on the floor.

A blood-curdling scream bursts from her mouth, triggering a domino effect in the rest of the crowd – then, pure silence. From somewhere off to her right a blur of black cloth slinks towards one of the speakers. Beacon collapses to the ground, hyperventilating. My EYE comes blaring to the forefront of my vision and my body surges with adrenaline. Materializing from the crowd, five men stand in a group, covered in black masks and holding samurai swords; one of the swords is covered in blood. If there was not so much adrenaline surging through my body, I would probably laugh. Death is only tragic for those who cannot fight it.

One second, two seconds, three seconds, then sheer panic ensues. Club Siv's trance is gone. People are screaming and running but behind Beacon, the gentlemen with the samurai swords are just standing there. The Being I identify as the leader is 6'2", unusually muscular even under his garments and has a blinking red dot in his cornea – his EYE. These are Beta Spikes, no doubt. He looks at me and smiles, but my smiles are gone for the night. Now is the time for action.

Leaping upwards, I push off the beer taps to propel myself off the bar and hurdle towards the formation of make-shift samurais. My spring was hard enough that I achieve enough momentum to pass clean over the group, simultaneously reaching down and snapping one of their necks. [Encounter: Target Executed. Targets Remaining: Four.] In less than a second, the remaining four scatter, taking their positions around me. They are moving at unusually fast speed for Beta Spikes as they zip through the onslaught trying to get out of the open doors.

One of the warriors darts forward but I snap a beer tap from the bar behind me and skewer him through the shoulder. He drops to the floor, writhing in pain as a trail of inky blood seeps from underneath his black garments. *Perfect Execution.* Grabbing a second tap, I bring it over my head to deliver the Executing blow but the fallen Beta charges at me – heaving his sword at me. He just misses my hamstring as I react, leaping into the air. Unfortunately, he stabs a passing Siv behind me. *That is so illegal it is not even funny.* Under what premise would the Country even allow this Encounter to happen in a club, much less with a majority of innocent Beings around?

Country regulations state that Sivs must have at least one minute to evacuate, or know the attack is coming beforehand. But I cannot dwell on what has already occurred and must use the moment of confusion to my advantage. [Search: Possible Weapons. Initiate. 3 objects found.] A loose bar on one of the Go-Go dancer's cage is the perfect option, how convenient. I spring towards the cage and grab the metal bar then twirl around, brandishing the bar like an ancient swordsman, thrusting it towards another one of the men. It catches him right above his nose and the metal bar plunges through his skull, emerging from the other side with brain stuck onto it. He immediately crumbles to the ground. *Well Executed.* [Encounter: Target Executed. Targets Remaining: Three.]

I move towards the remaining Beta and, even under the mask, I see the look of uncertainty in his eyes. He is ballsy and steps towards me anyway. I swing my bar and before I can impale it in his neck, the fallen Spike rises from behind, driving his sword through my calf muscle. *How, out of all the other places, was my calf muscle the easiest target?* My quad is double the size. He could have my chest or back – he could even cut off an arm – but instead, he chooses to go for my calf muscle? This makes me want to win even more badly.

My EYE reawakens, alerting me to a blood hemorrhage in my left gastrocnemius and soleus muscles. *As if I did not know.* If only I had received that notification earlier. But this type of blow gives me a clue that other, more inexperienced fighters would miss. No Alpha Spike would ever waste a blow on a calf muscle, so they definitely are Country-trained Beta Spikes unless England has their own program. *How ridiculous that would be.*

I grab the protruding sword and rip it out of my leg, causing a spit-back of blood on the man squirming on the ground. I forgot about him. I hold the samurai sword with both hands and bring it swiftly through his neck – like a steak knife through butter – severing his head from the rest of his body. This is so much fun. [Alert. Blood Concentration: Decreasing.] [Immediate Attention Required. Diagnostic Sent to Control. 3 Hours of Activity Remaining.] *Dammit, so I really cannot take my time with the remaining two of them?* [Encounter: Target Executed. Targets Remaining: Two.] The little baby Beta proceeds to come at me again. This time weaponless, but I am no longer in the mood.

The Spike grabs my hair and yanks my head backward, displacing my forward momentum. *Good move.* He grapples with the hilt of his sword, trying to regain ownership but once again I am too quick, snatching it out of his reach. I swing the sword around my head, like a whip from one of those old Western movies, and successfully take off the top layer of his skull. This won't be painful, but I know if he happens to escape and does not receive help soon, he will die from blood loss. I swerve out of the way of the oncoming warrior and let the Spike Execute him for me. *Bonus points!* [Encounter: Target Executed. Targets Remaining: One.]

The Spike, in his irrational and muddled state, tore the jaw off his partner, leaving him helpless.

I mercilessly plummet the sword through his heart.

All that is left is the baby Beta and me. We circle each other. He knows I have the upper hand. I can see it on his face. His face must be mimicking fear because Beta Spikes have no emotions either. *That is really good, he is really selling the fear.* We circle each other one more time and see the Queen's Guards who have rejoined my side. What minute are we on now? Four? Five? I wave them off; I need to finish this on my own. After all, I will probably receive a bonus from this Encounter.

I take the sword and toss it back at the Spike. Might as well make this as fair as I can because we both know he is finished. Confusion spreads across his face as the sword bounces toward him. His picks it up like it might explode but after a split second, he grips it and staggers towards me. Wow, he must have lost a lot of blood. The red dot in his eye is an oval. *EYEs are only circle shaped, is this new technology?* We spar for five seconds but the Spike soon falls to his knees, drops his sword and looks up at me. Every remaining Being in the club, including the members of my SQUAD, momentarily stop what they are doing. This is a video game to them. *What is going on right now?* Spikes fight until they are decapitated. This Beta, probably two years older than me, looks at me and I see water drip from the corner of his eyes.

There is something seriously wrong with this dude. A Spike is not meant to excrete water, only blood, unless … *no that is not possible*. There is a zero percent chance that this Spike has the ability to express genuine emotion. Spikes do not feel sadness. Only Sivs cry, right? Crying is represented by an outflowing of water from the nasolacrimal duct, and Spikes don't have them. I run this analysis through my EYE: [ERROR.] I ignore it. The Beta Spike is on his knees in front of me and now I see my image projected on every screen throughout the club. This is Primetime, if I do say so myself.

"They are after all of us. No one is supporting us anymore," the Beta says dramatically, blood coating his lips and dripping on the floor.

"What a sucker," I say, politely.

I bring the metal bar through the soft part of the neck, looking straight into his eyes as I do so. *He believes what he is saying.* Nevertheless, I pull the bar sideways; the Spike's head rolls to the opposite side and the weight of the head rips the remaining skin and tissue off his body. His head rolls off his shoulders and down his collapsed frame. Typically, I would not be so merciful, but his last comment slowed my reaction time, making me think instead of reacting, thus rendering me unable to accurately predict an incision point. I hate it when I cannot get an accurate puncture point. *I won't get as much money because it was a sloppy Execution.* [Encounter: Target Executed. Targets Remaining: N/A.] A pool of blood has started collecting around my Testoni shoes.

Four seconds tick by and then my audience erupts in cheers. The smile is back on my face, but I can't help but wonder what the Spike meant: "They are after all of us." Was he referring to the Sivs wanting to expel Countrians from England? Possibly. The Country is helping me. They allow Encounters to entertain the world, but other governments find it too cruel to partake in it themselves. *Nope, do not think about it.* I let the noise and the energy from the Sivs, my SQUAD, and Queen's Guard around me excite me back to a normal state. Molly comes running up behind me, slapping me on the back. *Since when has she been here? She said she was going to bed and staying at the palace.*

"Oh, Colman, you were absolutely wonderful, my dear. It is so unfortunate about poor Miss Torin but your Encounter went swimmingly. I cannot believe how valiantly you behaved and every Siv around the world is sending their compliments to our Keepers. But … before we go anywhere, we must get this post-Encounter briefing done so we can edit and air the segment for late-night. Are you ready?" she asks.

"As I will ever be, Molly."

"Wonderful! Gentlemen and ladies, he will now take your questions."

"Colman! Colman! Colman! Colman! Sir! What a performance I must say, do you think the alcohol had any influence on your Encounter? What happened to Marist and Vassar? Will you be alerting the Premier of Australia about Beacon's Execution? Who is in charge for organizing this attack? What will happen now that you do not have a woman to take home?"

I respond calmly. Molly must have been the one that coordinated this attack, right? That's her job, managing the Siv requests and then knowing when they are going to happen. With the way she is looking at me however, I can see that this came to her surprise as well. So ... who planned it? "Alcohol doesn't affect me, you should know that. Molly can answer all the rest of those questions for you."

I give her a look, wondering if she really can. She is excited but there is something else.

[Alert.   Blood   Concentration: 92%. Decreasing.] I have to make sure that is accounted for when I get back to the palace. I am about to leave when one reporter catches my attention.

"What did the Spike say to you before you Executed him?"

I turn, trying to get a good look at the reporter who just asked this question. The Queen's Guard swiftly removes this man from the room. *Strange, it was just a question.*

Molly finds me after the briefing is over and I am loaded back in my Bentley to depart for the palace. We arrive safely and I excuse myself from the Queen's Guard and thank them for their service. I walk down the long hallway back to my wing. Good on their promise, when I open the doors, I see that Bella and Roberto have the room is all set up for an Encounter. There are rose petals scattered over the floor, leading to the king size bed. The flicker of candles illuminates the ceiling and the pulled down silk sheets on the bed glimmer in the light.

"Not going to happen tonight, everybody," I say as I undress myself. I will not be able to sleep in the bed anyway; as a Spike, I must sleep in a glass tube with a variety of chemical lines hooked directly into my skin, to recharge myself.

Since 2025, sex repositioned itself in a societal and cultural acceptance. It became discussed after a lot of countries lost majorities of their populations. Since then, it has become the art form which it was always meant to be. Now all types of sexual acts and sexual deviances are popping up all over the globe. I am seen naked enough and there are tapes of my sexual Encounters in libraries and stores across the world. I like sex, because when I am having sex, I feel that same shot of adrenaline I get from killing.

Sex is meant to sustain or grow a population and give pleasure to the Beings partaking in it. However, I like to mix it up and if I can have a little bit of something 'extra' in it, I will not say no. Looking back around the room, I wonder if my ratings will drop because I didn't have a sexual Encounter tonight. Hopefully, my Encounter at the club should make up for that, but possibly not. I've noticed that Sivs derive different kinds of pleasure from watching me kill and watching me have sex.

My Entrance Tube, my hard bed, is the large glass cylinder that I was created in. It is cold, hard glass. Whenever I travel, I have to take this along with me in case, like today, I get injured during an Encounter. The Tube has monitors and repairing features that will heal and revive my physical structure. My calf, for example, will come out smooth as child's skin when I am awakened tomorrow morning. Whenever I enter the tube, I have to attach IVs to my body so I can restore to 100% capacity the next day. My calf muscle has already started to repair itself, but I lost a lot of fluids on my way back from the club.

I begin inserting my IVs, step into the Tube, and fall asleep thinking about what Marist was doing at The Globe and what the Spike meant when he said, *"They are after all of us"*.

CHAPTER 11

I awake the next morning as I have done every morning of my conscious life: Molly comes in, shuts off the oxygen flowing through the Tube and I am jolted awake by realizing I am suffocating. It is not as bad as it sounds because the physical stimulation revitalizes me, and I feel like I start everyday already having accomplished something – like making your bed.

I look up and see Molly scowling down at me.

"Bad news," she says.

"Yep, good morning to you too," I respond.

"Your ratings skyrocketed last night during the Encounter, but an English television channel broadcasted the Execution of the innocent Siv. Your Profile took a hit."

"How much of a hit are we talking? I have recovered from much worse. It can't be that bad."

"I know it was not your fault, but I got a call from a Keeper this morning saying that you lost your funds for today's outings."

"How is that a bad thing?" I shrug. They always give me my money back.

"Are you kidding me? I wanted to go out and explore London! We need money to do that! We need money for your camera team, money for security, money for the food, money for travel..."

"Were we supposed to do a lot today?" I ask. Her despair is fake and oh-so-dramatic.

"Yes! And now we can't. This day is off to such a bad start. We may leave tomorrow, but as of now we only have a budget of five million dollars. For the entire day!"

"Molly, do you listen to yourself when you talk? Five million dollars! That's enough to do anything we want."

"No, it is not," she whines.

"Yes, it is. Okay, how about this. Tell me what you wanted to do today, and I will make it happen for you."

She eyes me dubiously. "Really?"

"Yes, I will take over planning for today. You need a break anyways."

She smiles in genuine appreciation. "Here," she says as she hands me a clipboard.

Outlined are all the things 'she' wants to do. *I can't believe I fell for this again.* The list she gave me is only a ploy to get me out of Buckingham Palace and be seen with the princesses. This is all a trick to fix my Image. She smirks as she waits for me to read the list.

She is pretty funny. All of the things have to do with the princesses. *I bet she didn't even talk with any Keeper this morning.* I am being used so she can make more money. It figures.

"Molly, your request today to go picnicking by the Thames — you don't want to eat with me, you just want to watch?" I say.

"Yes, please continue."

"You also want to take a ride on the London Eye? No wait, you want me to take a ride while you stand below and watch me?" I smile.

"Yes, I do not like heights. Continue."

"You would like me to accompany you to The Globe to watch a performance of Romeo and Juliet, however, you want there to be two empty seats on either side of me and my companions while you watch from the back?"

"Yes, you really need your space, you are Famous, after all."

"I know exactly what you're doing. This is not sneaky…"

"You agreed that you would do this for me."

"But this has absolutely nothing to do with…"

"And if you would please direct your attention to the very last bullet point. This would make me very happy as well."

At the bottom of the sheet it says, 'I would like to have Vassar and Marist accompany me today. I heard they are wonderful young women and I want to get to know them better.'

I start laughing because this is such a ridiculous and obvious proposal, yet, she actually made it happen. She is the best and the worst at the same time.

"Fine, Molly, this is the last chance I am giving them. If Marist and Vassar do not make me look good today, then I will want to depart back for the Country – earlier than expected."

"Get it done," she says, and her eyes shrink as her mouth flattens into a fine line.

"Molly," I say as she turns to leave.

"Yes?"

"Did my Profile actually take a hit last night?"

"Check for yourself because I actually don't know. Alert me when you are ready to start the day. Thank you, Colman."

She leaves and I search for my EYE to see if my Image fell in rank last night. Sure enough, she's lying. I'm still number one, and my Profile views spiked right around the time of the murder.

My outfit for today consists of very English-style clothing. I grab a Versace shirt out of the wardrobe, pull out the high-waisted pants with suspenders, then reach for my tie and waistcoat, finishing it off with my Oxford Brogues and my cufflinks. I fit in perfectly with the English gentry. By the time I'm done, Fanto, Downey, Rosen and Cassidy are already outside. The Press is forcing their way through the open gates of the palace.

I show up to the massive gathering of my SQUAD and British reporters and notice that Marist and Vassar are looking as attractive as ever. Marist is wearing a yellow Dior original and Vassar is wearing a cream-colored Vera Wang.

"Colman! Who did you end up sleeping with last night? Colman! How did all the cameras turn off last night? Have you been Repaired? Did you shut the cameras off last night? Did you sneak in a princess? Sir!

We heard that there is a possibility of an early departure, is that true? Colman! What happened this morning? Did you hear about Mr. Torin's reaction to the death of his Recipient? What happened to all of you last night?"

I barely have enough time to respond before Marist starts speaking.

"Members of the Press: to the best of my knowledge, Colman has just woken up and I would prefer if we started this day off on a good foot. If you are disrespectful now, I will be disappointed for the rest of the day and none of you want an angry princess. If the princess is angry then you do not get to ask any of these frivolous questions to begin with. Are we clear?"

The cameras stop flashing and the reporters are holding their recording devices in the air even though Marist has stopped talking. They all look a little shell-shocked.

"Very well then. If you would excuse us, we are off for the day. If anyone of you gets within fifty feet of myself, my sister, or Mr. Cai, I will be sure to make the Queen's Guard stop you by any means necessary."

A cheer emits from the Press and Marist simply smiles then tucks her head to the side to hide the majority of her face from the cameras.

"That one is a keeper," Downey says, tapping me.

"A Keeper?" I say.

"Not a Keeper from the Country, more like ... it is an old-world saying meaning ... never mind."

I shrug.

"I believe you are all riding in the same car this morning," Downey says.

"That can't be right."

"I'm just telling you what I was told."

What a special occasion!

Downey and Rosen take the lead with Cassidy and Fanto following behind. My security is back and looking good; the fierce Queen's Guard is there, too—overkill, if you ask me. There are only five cars in the procession for this afternoon's outings so Downey must be correct. My SQUAD and the press will take two of them, the Queen's Guard will take one, as will my security, which leaves one for the remaining three people. Molly is smiling with two big thumbs up from the top of the stairs. She is betting that I will break this contract, she may even want me to. She is pushing me closer and closer to these girls. She is a stickler for following the Country's regulations but what she wants in this world, more than anything else, is the money. All she really cares about is ratings. She'll tell me to follow rules, she'll insist it's the most important thing, but if my ratings drop, she'll forget all that in a hot second. She wants to be the one who built and developed an Alpha Spike, skyrocketing it to the top. And the funny thing is, she thinks I have no idea.

Marist and Vassar are escorted down by their prospective teams. Vassar looks miserably hungover and Marist looks tired. Whatever she was doing last night really sucked the life out of her. Vassar brushes by me and does not say a word. *Crap, so now both of them dislike me.* Although she looks exhausted, Marist seems to have donned a different personality for today.

"Colman, you are with us. We are sorry that we caused a stir last night, so as repayment our Fame team decided the narrative should be reconstructed."

"How kind of them," I sigh. They do not care about being with me, this decision – as always – is directed by the potential profit. I move out of the way as she slides onto the leather seats. Her dress drapes perfectly over her legs and I quickly decide to give a final wave to the fans so I can avoid looking at her smooth skin.

"You're the reason the PM's daughter is dead," Vassar says outright. "You are a pig, Colman. Always looking out for number one. I should have known."

"Vassar, please, do we really have to start off this way?" Marist chimes in but the way she smirks, I can tell she plans to milk this.

"Shut up, Marist."

"Vassar, that is very unfair."

"No, do you know what is unfair? The fact that I stuck it out through the entire night last night and you disappeared the minute you entered the club. That was not the agreement."

"Whoa, ladies, please. If I can just explain what happened, as it is obvious you already know," I interject.

"Why *Beacon Torin*? What does she have that I don't have?" Vassar asks.

"Nothing. She's dead," I mutter. I can't believe this. She is jealous of a dead woman.

"Vassar, compose yourself," Marist scolds.

"Look. I go where I'm told to go. It's a ratings thing. And I was told that I needed to be with Beacon. That's all. My SQUAD would tell you the same thing. You can confirm these events with them."

"Thank you for clearing that up, Colman." Marist adds, "Vassar thought you didn't want her anymore."

"I knew it wasn't true," Vassar sulks.

"Great, so now that's all cleared up, I have a question for you, Marist," I say.

"And that is?"

"Where did you go last night?"

Her composure flickers for a millisecond. After years of learning to understand and identify emotions in Sivs, a millisecond is all I need. She is fearful, guilty, but also hopeful.

"I went to meet some friends who were in town," Marist responds but Vassar looks at her skeptically.

"And they were in the club?" I say.

"Yes, they were in the back."

"No, she's lying," Vassar says. "Ever since we found out your trip was planned, Marist has been sneaking off at random times of the day and night, showing up the next morning looking like she rolled in the mud."

"That's not true!" Marist yells.

"Yes, it is! Why are you not going to admit this?" Vassar responds.

"It is not true," she says again and then she turns to me. "Colman, you saw me go to the VIP area last night did you not?"

"Yes, but…"

"Discussion over. Vassar, really, stop being so suspicious. We have to enjoy today, and I will not be able to do that if we start it like this."

"Fine," Vassar sulks.

"Great, now, Colman, unless there is anything else, I think we should all put on some music and sit in silence and just get through the day. Unless someone," she says pointedly looking at her sister, "has any better ideas?"

"Play your music. I don't care. I'm not going to listen to it anyways."

Besides the music, we sit in silence the rest of the way. I try to strike up a conversation with the princesses, but Marist looks like she is sleeping, and Vassar is immersed in her Profile. I finally get to have a car ride with other Beings but I am still completely isolated.

The day goes by with reasonable ease. Vassar at least knows how to flash a smile for a crowd, even if deep down I know she's hungover and tired and seething. Marist's whole demeanor has changed. For a while I think she is happy to be around me, and then I realize how stupid I'm being: it's all for the photos. The Image. The Press. The Fame.

We finish our day with a visit to The Globe to see a Shakespeare play. I'm exhausted of being trotted out for the masses by now, but Marist still looks flawless. How does she do it? Why do I keep noticing these things about her?

And what is that feeling in my stomach when I do?

"So…do either of you like Shakespeare?" I say as we wait for the Press to prepare themselves for our entrance into the theater.

"Uh, I hate it. What is the point of going to the theater if someone is not being Executed?" Vassar retorts.

"I think he is brilliant. There is a lot to be said for someone who is willing to dedicate his life to writing stories solely for the enjoyment of others," Marist says.

"And what are we seeing?" I ask. I know the answer, but I want to make some type of headway with these two. I pick up my drink and start sipping it to make the question seem casual and nonchalant.

"Romeo and Juliet. Have you ever heard of it before?" Marist asks.

Crap. I choke on my drink because Marist must think very low of me if she believes I have never heard of Romeo and Juliet before. The surprise makes me spit the contents of my mouth all over the front of Marist's dress. *There goes my headway.* Marist pulls back while slapping me at the same time.

"What was that for?" she yells. Vassar is laughing and pushes me out of her way so the same thing will not happen to her.

"I am not letting that happen to me in this dress. I am getting out," she says as she straddles me. "Colman this is what you could have had last night, but instead you went for the dead Australian. Too bad."

She then grabs my throat, leans in for a kiss, and at the last second, exits the car.

"Marist, I am so sorry. I don't know what happened," I stammer.

"Colman, it's fine. I am the sorry one. I know you know what Romeo and Juliet is, I don't even know why I said that. Obviously, you're not like Vassar and the others. It was foolish of me. I just need to get out of this dress."

"Let me help you," I say a little too quickly. She laughs ... *is that a rebuke or confirmation?*

"So I suppose this was on purpose? You spit your drink on me so I have to physically shed the clothes I am wearing?"

"No not at all, ma'am," I stutter. *Ma'am?*

She looks at me like she is about to say something then shakes her head.

[111]

"Then what you can do is escort me out of this car and into the bathroom, where you will leave once you have safely escorted me in. This will give both of our Images a boost and ignite a Press flurry that will carry us through the rest of the night. This way we do not need any other major events to happen, got it?"

"Ah, so was this your plan all along? Making me spit my vodka on you so I have to escort you into the bathroom where I will … not watch you undress?"

"Shut up and help me out of the car," she snorts.

I open the door and am greeted with the usual flood of light. My security already knows what happened inside the car and that I will be the one escorting Marist inside. I plant my feet firmly outside the door and hoist my body up and out of the window seat. I see Marist shuffle her legs and get a brief appearance of her lace underwear. *What I wouldn't give…*

She is ready to get out and as I reach out to grab her, she jolts up and into my arms. *Did time just move in slow motion or did my vision just speed up?* Either way, this is not the time to dwell on this minor detail. I put my hand up to block the flashes as the cameras click, while reaching for hers to guide her safely inside. Marist is also covering her face and is keeping with my step as we make our way into the theater. No, Marist is pulling me along into the theater. I must look like I am a dog on a leash! *How is this girl doing this?*

[112]

We reach the theater entrance and are greeted by the Director and a few of the actors, telling us how glad they are that we arrived to see their performance. Marist thanks them and shows them her dress. A few of the women screech and pretend to care about her, while the males in the cast are smirking at me with raised eyebrows. I try to brush them off and tell them it is not like that but her effect on them is obvious.

"So, is this about how far I take you?" I ask, once we get into the bathroom.

"No, you need to come in."

"But you are here safely…" I start.

"Colman, come," she demands.

Confused, I take a step in the bathroom and the door clicks behind us. Unsure of what else to do, I turn to leave but she grabs my arm and throws herself at me. She pushes me against the wall, and we slide along the tiled surface until we find ourselves in the corner near one of the stalls. Her lips are on mine and I do not remember if I have ever been more attracted to someone. Her red lipstick is already smeared all over my bottom lip and she tastes incredible. It is like drinking rosewater – subtle but very sweet. When I think I cannot handle anymore, her hands pull my hair so that my ear rests near her mouth. She has a death grip on me. I try to kiss her, but she whispers to me instead.

"You can pretend like you are kissing me, but I need you to listen."

Woah, what?

[113]

"There are some things you need to know. Things that have been going on recently that no one is going to tell you, but you must know before it is too late."

Utterly bewildered by what is happening, I try to kiss her; *she told me to kiss her didn't she?* I feel her shiver slightly and all of her weight falls into my arms, my knees give way but her grip in my hair is so tight that she holds me by my head.

"Colman, listen."

"What's going on?" I say, breathlessly.

"I need to tell you something - we have to be in the corner so the microphones cannot hear us."

If this was in the Country, this Encounter would border on the line of inappropriate. We are not in an approved location for an Encounter such as this. A violation of this rule is definitely going to get us in trouble. That is what I have repeatedly been told. This time is so different. Her mouth is so close to the soft part of my neck and somewhere deep from within me makes me shift so she touches it with her lips. But the desperation in her voice overrides everything. I recover from the physical sensation of whatever just happened and feel my heart beating powerfully in my chest. She pushes me back then slams me against the wall, so hard that more tiles fall off. Why is this girl so strong?

"Colman, listen, you are going to be Executed in England if you don't leave soon."

"That's impossible," I say as she holds my head near her mouth.

"That is what they want you to think. You think that as an Alpha you are invincible, but it's not true. They can kill you when they want to. And you are now their target," she says quietly. "They want to."

"No, Marist listen to me," I say as I try to make some space between us, "Whoever told you this is wrong. The Country is protecting me. This is just one big publicity tour. I am here to make money and nothing else."

"You're wrong," she pleads. "You have to get out of England and make sure you go to a different State that protects Spikes."

"Marist, are you ok? This is alarming. Did something happen last night?" I question.

She releases her grip on my head and instead grabs my arms. She picks me up and hurtles me through one of the bathroom stalls. I fly the length of the bathroom and try to regain my balance, but she is already holding me on the other side. I try to connect with my EYE but the only thing I can see on the screen are the words 'Turn ON".

I don't get it. I never turned it off.

A sharp rattling on the door echoes throughout the bathroom. Marist, the spider monkey, places me back down in the opposite corner and I stare at her in disbelief.

"Don't worry, any cameras in here are shut off. I scoped this out last night."

"What? Why were you here last night? How did you just do that?"

"Exactly for this reason and I will have to explain later," she says. "We cannot talk about this anymore; my security team will come in soon."

She pushes me off her and tells me to get out. It feels like my head has fallen off my body and I am holding it in my hands. Is this a dream? But no, I see her, and I see the rest of the bathroom. Definitely not a dream. She fixes her dress in the mirror and reapplies her makeup. She looks at me and heads toward the door but pauses and takes a deep breath before facing the Press's ambush. Opening the door, with the most innocent smile on her face, the space fills with light. Her smile broadens and she does a little hair flip as she disappears through the slit. My EYE somehow comes back online, and I see a live shot of Marist and a headline: "Romeo and Juliet see Romeo and Juliet: Colman and Marist Have a Quickie in The Globe's Bathroom."

A second knock on the door catapults me back to reality. Fanto pokes her head in and asks if everything is ok. She notices that I am out of it and gives me a puzzled look before coming all the way in – something is wrong. Her eyes drop and she closes the door behind her as she enters.

"We are prepared for anything," she says, handing me new clothes. There are blood drops on my shirt from where I hit the tile.

"Thank you, Fanto," I mutter.

"Are you physically able to walk?" she adds almost jokingly.

"Yes, I'm fine. Is Marist seated already? How long was I in here?"

"About four minutes."

"Ok," I mutter, still in a daze. "Then I better get out there."

"Sir are you sure you are ok?" she asks looking at me quizzically.

An emotion registers on her face, one that is not supposed to appear on any member of my security detail's face: compassion. For some unknown reason, my autopilot kicks in and I get ready to fight.

"Totally fine, yep, thank you for checking on me. She was a wild ride. That's one for the history books for sure," I say bluffing my way towards the door.

She knows something is wrong, but she does not push me. She escorts me into the flashing lights, and I emerge from the women's bathroom, getting a lot of snickers and death stares from other patrons in the theater. I walk down the center aisle to find my reserved seat in the front. All eyes are on Marist and me when I sit down next to her. Do people think I am going to do something?

"I am so over you, Colman. Marist, you said you didn't find him attractive and then you did that," Vassar pouts and then immerses herself in her Profile.

The five-minute warning for the show chimes in the theater and the cameras are asked to leave. I sit down next to Marist and see her glance sideways. For the first time all morning, I have a chance to use my

EYE. Was Molly bluffing about my performance last night? So much has happened since then, but my Fame is the only topic that can distract me from the thought of Marist sitting so close next to me. My EYE shows an incredible 11-point increase in ratings.

CHAPTER 12

The show goes well. It was an incredible performance, and, at such an iconic theater, it was memorable beyond belief. I couldn't help my paranoia though. I was half expecting one of the actors to throw themselves from the stage to attack me, after hearing what Marist said, but nothing of the sort came to be. At the finale, I was glad to get out of the theater because the Sivs had started taking pictures of Marist and me sitting next to each other and we were getting awfully close.

The three of us – Marist, Vassar, and myself – regroup with our teams so we can be briefed on what activity is next. We exit the theater and walk towards the processions of cars waiting for us. My SQUAD is following behind Marist and me, wanting to get more B-roll for tonight, while Vassar lags behind talking to some male Siv. Security is following at a reasonable pace and ... *wait, my security never gives me this much space.* Do they know that another attack is coming?

We are about to exit the theater when I feel a tap on my shoulder, I spin around and twist the arm that just touched me. Cassidy looks like he is in pain, but he is trying his best not to scream.

"Sir, the theater staff just went into the women's bathroom and are not pleased with what they saw."

"What did they see?" I say.

"They said that the stalls were destroyed, and it looked like a body had been thrown against the wall."

Wasn't Fanto supposed to take care of that?

"Tell them I will pay for the repairs," I say.

"Sir, you do not understand. They want to press charges against you for allegedly throwing Marist through the wall. Sir, I may be understating this. It's serious. Because they think you hurt the princess, they are motioning to hold you in the Embassy tonight."

"What? You cannot be serious," I say, shocked. "Marist is here. She is fine. She doesn't have a scratch on her."

"Sir, I am sorry."

"Has anyone asked Marist what happened here?"

"Sir, we tried that already, but they are saying that you could have threatened her to stay silent."

"How dare they think I assaulted my hosts! I admit something obviously happened but how come they are so quick to press charges? I mean I am with the princesses of England, there must be some way to get out of this. The queen must have at least a little power left?"

"Sir, it was the queen who filed for your capture."

There is that word again! No one can capture me. I was designed to Execute and be un-capturable. That old hag-bag, million-year-old witch does not even know what she is dealing with right now. I did not know she was so petty.

Marist groans. "Oh, bloody hell."

"You can talk sense into her?" I ask.

She shakes her head. "Likely no. Once she gets an idea in her head... I can do nothing."

"Let me get this straight. I am going to be ... captured," the word is a nasty taste in my mouth, "because there have been allegations that I threw the princess through the wall?"

"Yes."

"What if she threw me against the wall and through the stalls? Would there be any problem?"

"Sir, that is not a very good hypothetical question."

Little do you know.

I turn to tell Marist the news and she apologizes but we both know that whatever happened in there, it cannot be shared with the world – no matter how much I want to. There are so many questions. Vassar looks overjoyed that I am leaving, and she signals a final 'screw you' before slipping into her car.

"Colman I am so sorry this had to happen. There is so much I need to tell you, but you must promise me that you will not say anything to anyone about what we discussed."

"I promise."

"I am going to try to convince my grandmother to let you out tomorrow morning but by then the Country will have already made plans for you to leave. I know this does not help with your Image, but it will be worth it later on. Farewell and see you shortly." She leans in and kisses me on the cheek.

Really, would she have done that if I'd thrown her through the wall.

Fanto and Rosen push the princess away from me. My head is a little fuzzy now. Downey and Cassidy start to pull me backward making the gap between Marist and me larger. A flurry of activity separates us, and I am hoisted away from her. The place where she kissed me is tingling. The Queen's Guards' eyes collectively widen under their helmets and they surge towards Marist, ripping her from the growing space between us. My heart feels weird. The car screeches to a halt and Marist is thrown in – not gently, literally thrown - but she does not break eye contact with me the entire time. There is a buzzing in the back of my brain. Security is now running some type of diagnostic test on their Phase 1 EYEs and are still panicking. The car's doors shut, and Marist is again out of view. Downey and Cassidy are still holding me locked in their arms and Molly jumps into my EYE.

"Colman get in the car! You just broke Country Regulation on an international scale with what you did at The Globe. All the Keepers are now scrambling to remove those signals from the network. I do not think you know the gravity of the situation you just put yourself in."

"Molly," I respond but she is already gone. I feel physically numb; the back of my brain is ticking. I look down and try to move my fingers, but nothing happens. It is like my brain is being controlled by some other mechanism. My Rolls pulls up and out of it jumps Molly who hands Downey a syringe of ... blood? Is that for me? I try to get a closer look, but she takes the needle and pulls out a blue liquid, similar to the color of my eyes. She looks at me and then jabs it into my neck.

The ticking in my brain recedes and all the physical sensations I just felt retreat as quickly as they came. My SQUAD is completely turned around, physically blocking my circle from the rest of the crowd. It is almost as if they are trying not to witness something illegal. I am getting notifications from Keepers and Producers all around the globe, pertaining to Country regulation, but whatever Downey just injected into my neck is putting me to sleep. A long black car eases into view. The back door is opened, and I am guided towards the darkness.

In the car is someone who has held Power for a very long time. He could have not picked a better time but why is he here? The last thing I remember is Kendall Khan's perfect white teeth illuminating the interior of the car for a split second, and then I fall unconscious.

CHAPTER 13

There are very few things I have seen or experienced that will stay with me for the rest of my life: major Executions, my first Press conference, meeting my security team and stylists, when I discovered I had my own private jet and then, the gleaming-white and flawless smile of Kendall Khan. I know for a fact that smiling is a forced reaction because he is a severe and serious man, but he executes it perfectly.

By the time I come to, I am in my Embassy. It is funny to think that embassies are meant to places of refuge because I wake up in mine strapped to a chair. However, while this may seem extreme to you, this happens to me probably more than it should – for good and bad reasons.

There is a plate of tea and cookies on a table in front of me and I am situated in a very nicely furnished room with curtains hugging the window frames and a plush carpet beneath my feet. There is real sunlight coming in from outside, not that fake sunlight they use during an interrogation.

Wait – sunlight? How long have I been out? Is it seriously tomorrow already?

One member of my security team is situated in each corner of the room and they are trying to avoid eye-contact.

"Ah, superboy awakens. It is so very nice to see you," Khan says from behind me.

Kendall Khan was the leader of the Democratic Republic of the Congo but is now Super of the Country. The Congo is no longer democratic, a republic, or even the Congo after he was through with it. Stories say that Khan was raised by a family of leopards because his parents abandoned him. Of course that was a lie; he grew up in a very wealthy family that oversaw diamond mining in South Africa. He attended a military school where he was top of his class until he was deployed for the Iraq War to help fight a terror group in search of weapons of mass destruction.

Before it was called the Country, it was called the United States of America. Khan discovered that he could make a substantial profit during wartime so instead of fighting terror groups and searching for WMDs, he created his own terror group and stole the WMDs that the USA found in Iraq. After establishing himself as the name of terror, he started developing and distributing WMDs to any State willing to pay a premium. This man is a business genius and does not have a kind bone in his body. We get along well - even when he is torturing me.

"Khan, it is my absolute pleasure. Now, are we going to jump into the fun stuff or are we going to talk for a bit while we wait for the queen to arrive?"

"You think she is coming?" he asks, almost kindly.

"You forget that an EYE can tell me anything."

I knew Cassidy was not supposed to tell me that the queen ordered my capture so instead of causing unnecessary pain upon him I play it off cool.

"Oh, Colman, you really think the queen ordered that you be taken here? You think she had anything to do with this?"

What?

"The queen answers to me, Colman, you should know that. And I wanted you here. Can you guess why?"

I try to regain my composure. "Of course."

"So tell me – why am I here?" he grins.

"First off, you are here to congratulate me on seducing both princesses even though I did not sleep with them. Secondly, you are here to tell me that this is all a big mistake. Third, you are here to kiss my ass. Isn't that right?"

"You really are something, Colman. However, not correct," he says drolly. "I am here to enforce the regulations of the Country. It's important that no Siv out there feels as if they have any personal freedom. That would be disastrous. For your insubordination – carrying out an unauthorized tryst and then throwing that poor girl into a wall – I am going to broadcast your torture. I am sorry to have to do this to you, but the Country needs to see what happens to those who do not

[126]

obey. None of this is personal, Colman, but you should know your place by now. You may have killed every opponent you've ever come up against, but your ass is mine, and this is a reminder that I can end you whenever I please. Lower the walls please," he directs.

Well, this ought to be fun.

On cue, the room I was sitting in opens to the English countryside. The walls around me fall over like some strong wind blew them down and the very pleasant sunlight envelops me. Khan comes around the front of me with his sunglasses on.

"I like your style. Are those RayBans?" I say.

"Why yes, they are. How astute."

"Thank you. Did you know RayBan just endorsed me? I could probably get you a free pair if you want."

"I can get a free pair anytime I want."

"Fine. Have it your way," I smirk.

The sunlight is so bright I cannot see anything in front of me. I feel the coolness of metal as a knife emerges from somewhere behind my head. It taps the spot right where Marist kissed me. *I wish I could feel her now.*

I was mistaken thinking I had actually been taken to my Embassy. I am sitting in an open field in the English countryside. It does not intimidate me. Fear is associated with negative outcomes of previously experienced situations. I think the Keepers who organized this Encounter for Kendall forget that none of this grand spectacle actually gets to me. It makes for better ratings, drama always equates to higher ratings, but it is so unnecessary to put me in a box in the woods.

The metal edge of the knife pushes against my cheek and my beautiful skin splits open, blood filling in the surface. I try to catch some in my mouth to spit at Kendall but no such luck.

I feel another incision open on the side of my neck. Is this just a coincidence or is that the exact spot Marist kissed me?

Twenty-eight seconds and counting.

Kendall comes back in front of me and is holding his knife like a Siv holding candy. He takes the tip and puts it to my quad and pushes a little bit. Then he takes the tip and moves it a millimeter over. *Twenty seconds.*

"Are you really trying to draw a crown?" I ask.

"I think you deserve it. It looks like the princesses played with your head."

"You are messed up, dude," I say.

"I know."

He seems a bit exasperated that I'm not moaning in pain or crying for him to stop. His fault. If he wanted to show the world his power by having me cower in fear in front of him, he picked the wrong guy. I couldn't do it, even if I wanted to.

Fourteen seconds. He finishes his blood drawing of a crown, then steps back to examine his work. It does not even look like a crown. Good thing he is a dictator and not an artist. *Ten seconds*. He brings the knife back up to my face and lets my blood drip onto its metallic surface. Interesting choice but something about this gesture is not okay; my body surges with adrenaline as he smiles down on me. I hope that is not what I look like when I Execute people. *Five seconds.*

"So, what should we use next Colman? I have a hammer, I think," Khan taunts.

Four seconds.

"I don't think you're going to have time to use another weapon," I smirk.

Three seconds.

"And where will you be going?" he says, his eyes flickering with slight fear.

Two seconds.

"You have taken too long and I want to get out of here."

One second.

[Initiate: Weapons Search: 8 objects found.]

"You really think…" he starts.

Enough talking; I am tired of this game. I already rely on a 100% blood capacity to function normally, which means if I waste any more blood, then the money allocated elsewhere for this tour must be repurposed to find me more blood donors. That is not what I am about to do.

Kicking my right leg up, connecting with the Super's crotch, I use all my strength to push outward against the binds. He crouches over in pain and lets go of the knife. These people are seriously so stupid. Why would someone not think to tie my legs to the chair? *Have none of these people watched any spy movie ever made?* The knife skids across the floor and Fanto lunges for it but I quickly tip myself over and use Khan's body to propel my momentum towards the knife.

Fanto instantly retreats, if she grabs the knife, she will be violating her orders to never interfere in an Encounter. I grab the knife and successfully cut off the duct tape holding my right arm. *Nope, not quick enough, Colman.* Khan is already back up. He looks furious which makes me laugh. I don't understand why he would have put himself in this position. Do these people never learn?

Khan, looking like a crazed psychopath, comes racing at me and grabs the chair I was previously sitting in. He brings it hard over my head and because he is not fully recovered, he wavers when the chair is out of his grasp. I take this chance and swipe at him, but he backs away. Once I successfully cut my left arm out of the tape, my security exits the Encounter space because they know it is going to get a lot messier. Khan is still standing but for a man people think was raised by leopards he looks scared.

"You stupid idiot! You don't do anything you're told!" Khan growls.

"I am doing you a favor. You should be thanking me," I say as I threaten Khan with the knife.

"How is that?" he sneers.

"Isn't playing this out for the world to see highly detrimental to the Country's reputation? Torturing your own people gets most leaders killed," I remind him. "Especially one who can't be afraid of you."

"I do what I want."

"You should listen to me if you want your life," I threaten.

He pauses and I expect to see some semblance of fear, but his expression is one of pure elation. He is expecting some sort of reaction from me.

"Then Execute me."

"Fine," I say with a final shrug.

I lunge towards Khan. He blinks twice but otherwise doesn't move. It seems as though he wants to die. I am in the air for two seconds and I focus all my strength to make sure that I plunge the sharp blade into his body. Just before the tip of my knife strikes his throat, my entire hand swerves and the knife magically redirects towards the floor. *What the ...* I pull back and switch hands. The same thing happens. He has not moved. He is standing there smiling, nonchalantly picking at the cuticles on his fingers.

"You forget that I am the one who keeps you alive. You think I would not have implanted a code that would secure my safety from a monster like you? You must be more stupid than I thought."

"That is impossible. I am not some coded computer. I am a living Being," I say.

"Then try again," he says, indicating the knife sitting useless in my hands.

I lunge at him again but my hand swerves before making contact. He starts laughing,

"Poor Spike. I own you. Or do you not remember? I made you what you are today, and I can, and will, take that away when and where I please."

"No, that is not possible," I murmur. "You control my Encounters, not my free will."

"What a shame you didn't realize this earlier. Did you ever wonder how your handler knows what you're thinking before you do?"

"Molly doesn't control me either," I say.

"Doesn't she? Isn't that her job? She has an EYE that sees into your every thought. Haven't you ever wondered why she knows everything you're about to do, even before you do it?"

I frown, breathing hard, trying to make sense of this admission. Does she?

"It's always a tumultuous day when a Spike realizes that he or she has no self-control. You are a monster. You are not one of us."

"Right. I am *more* than you!" I yell.

"But you are not. I made you in a lab from two donors who were forced to give themselves up for your benefit. We broke you down and built you up into whatever we wanted. You're nothing but a freak."

"This is not true."

"Then try Executing me again."

I do not even bother this time as Khan turns his back to me and heads towards the car that has just pulled up, waiting to take him back to the airport.

"Oh, Colman, touché on getting out of this interrogation. Just remember it is only because I let you." He saunters toward his waiting car. "Please give my best to the queen when you see her. I'm sure we will see each other when you return from this little trip of yours. Thanks for your time and remember that I am always watching you."

No, they cannot own me.

I own me. They can try to kill me, but they cannot possibly control everything about me. I am not some video game. Kendall smiles as he gets into the car, dismissing my security from their posts to attend to me. He did not take me out here to interrogate me. This was a big ploy so he could intimidate me and show me that I cannot harm him.

But why now?

CHAPTER 14

My security approaches me like I am an injured newborn animal.

But I'm not even that. I may bleed, but I'm not one of them. I am a computer, with no mind of my own.

Did they know this about me?

How can I know if my actions are controlled by someone else? What if my thoughts are programmed for a specific outcome and my proceeding actions are the product? Surely that's not possible. Only one thing is for certain: Khan came all this way to make a point and he set me up so I would try to kill him. And if that's the case, does that mean that what Marist told me is true too? Khan broadcast me trying, and failing, to kill him. I look weak and he looks stronger than ever.

As we walk towards the cars, a rustling from a nearby brush catches my attention. [Targets Identified: One.] Khan sent someone to spy on me.

"Wait for me in the car, I left something back there," I say, taking a few steps back towards the sound.

I run around the outcropping of trees, but his spy is already moving away from me. I will not let him survive. I only see the outline of a shadow, but it is enough for me to track it. Breaking into a sprint as I make my way towards the shape, my body kicks into an overdrive that I did not know existed. *What about the last Encounter is making me act like this?* I have never felt like this before. As I hurdle through the thicket, leaves and twigs cutting into my face [Targets: One. Identified. Direction: SW] I recognize that the figure is moving at an equal speed to myself. *Khan sent a Beta to watch me.*

Bursting through the final section of woods, peering through the leaves and shrubbery to lock onto my target, I cannot believe what I am seeing. *How the Spike did she get out here?* Marist doesn't notice that I followed her but is cruising at a speed unimaginable. This has to be a dream.

I look around for a car, or at least another Being, thinking that her transport must be somewhere near because the palace would never let a princess traverse the countryside unprotected. I use my EYE to search for heat signatures of other Beings, but the result tells me that no one else is around. In utter disbelief, I don't pay attention to where I'm going and trip on a log, cursing loudly as I do. Marist looks behind her; her hair flows around her shoulders and her eyes pierce the surrounding area almost as if they are emitting light.

Her eyes widen, not in fear but in anticipation, then she bolts for cover. *She cannot hide anymore.* [Outbound Message. Recipients: SEC DETAIL. Message 1. You are going to have to wait another twenty minutes. Send. Message 2. Do not leave the car.] Marist is still in my direct line of sight as I weave through the woods, both of us sprinting deeper into the countryside. On my Entrance Day, the Keepers tested my speed and I clocked out at fifty-five miles per hour, but Marist is running even faster than that. *How is that possible?*

One of the things I quickly realized about top predators is that they believe no one is hunting them. The thing about me is that I have been hunted since the day I was born.

[Diagnostic Test. Begin. Motion Sensor: Active subject. Speed 33 MPH. Moving SW.]

I am truly pushing myself. I haven't opened my legs like this in a run for a very long time and it feels like an animal is awakening inside of me

[Diagnostic Test. Initiate. Temperature: Registers at 100 degrees Fahrenheit.]

[Diagnostic Test. Initiate. Blood Analysis: Subject. Alive. Blood Type. Inconclusive.]

Why is that showing up like that?

[Diagnostic Test. Initiate. Perceived Exertion. Subject: Approx. 10 Points.]

[Diagnostic Test. Initiate. Blood Pressure: 130/85.]

[Diagnostic Test. Initiate. Respiration Rate: Elevated. 26-28 Breaths/Minute.]

[Diagnostic Test. Initiate. Pulse Rate: 100 BPM.]

How does she have normal vitals? She is moving faster than the speed of a thoroughbred racehorse. Marist swivels her head for a second time, to see if I am still following her, and her face cracks into the most delicious, knowing smile. She slows down momentarily and after an initial moment of confusion, I realize she is taunting me. *She wants me to catch her!* Stretching my legs even farther, her smile falters as I close in on my target.

We are locked in at the same speed. My displacement is showing that I have traveled almost two miles since I started chasing after her and I know that I cannot keep this up for much longer. A whiff of her perfume drifts past me as I approach.

[Distance to Target: 50 feet.]

[Distance to Target: 30 feet.]

[Distance to Target: 20 feet.]

My knees wobble ever so slightly as the sweet smell floats past me. [Distance to Target: 5 feet.]

She yells at me as I am about to catch her, "You are going to have to do a lot better than this if you want to get anywhere near me! See you back at Buckingham Palace." And with that, she sprints away.

My speedometer trained on her surges from 25 MPH to 105 MPH and then my EYE loses range.

Speechless, I try to watch where she is headed but I get a large red notification on my EYE that a landmine is approaching and I swerve to avoid it. I am almost three miles away from security. Twenty minutes after my departure, I get notifications from Molly and all four of my main team asking what happened. I said that I saw a Pronghorn when I went back to collect my belongings and had to follow it. Molly says she'll see me at the palace for dinner and then signs off from her Communication software.

"Pronghorn, my ass," Cassidy says.

"I know for a fact that Pronghorns only roam in the Country under the protection of the Game Patrol," chimes in Downey.

"There are no Pronghorns in England," adds Rosen.

Maybe they are more educated than I originally thought. *Damn.*

"Even if I was not chasing a Pronghorn…"

"Which you weren't," says Fanto.

"But if I was that is not for you to ask me … is it?"

"Sir," Downey says, "We are here to make sure you do not get hurt in any unnecessary ways. If you were indeed chasing after a Pronghorn, then that would be considered an unnecessary danger. Technically we should ask you."

"Then let us all, for my sake and for yours, agree that what I saw was a Pronghorn. There is no other reason I would have wandered off for that long."

I feel like an adult Siv scolding the children. They load into the car and we set off towards Buckingham Palace. Halfway through the commute, I realize that this is the second time in two days that I have been allowed to ride with other Beings. I can see on their faces that they still feel guilty, so I ask the driver to put on some music. They are not usually allowed to listen to music because it is a privilege reserved for the extremely wealthy, but I figure they can use the diversion. To my surprise, they disregard all protocol and start humming to the music for the entirety of the ride back.

They sober up once we return to Buckingham Palace, as I am greeted by the Press who have finalized the editing for my torture video. They cannot show the Super letting me go. Instead, the propaganda is basically a dramatic video cutting in and out of the physical mutilation. Even though the Images make me uncomfortable and will most definitely lower my ratings, I have to give credit where credit is due – it's good footage.

The queen is coming down from her royal chamber as I enter the palace doors. She is in her best jewels and nicest dress and she pauses as she passes to slide her hand across my bloody face, tsking, before making her way into the dining room. Molly comes down after the queen, talking to someone on her invisible earpiece and passes me without saying anything. Am I invisible to her?

I run to my wing with my SQUAD and security behind me … interesting that my SQUAD is back. I wonder what happened to them after they caught Marist kissing my cheek. It is not their fault, obviously, but I know they had to have been punished somehow. I will certainly not receive any more privacy in the next twenty-four hours because they are going to try to get back in good graces with the Keepers and make up for lost footage.

Bella and Roberto have laid out my clothes on my bed which helps tremendously. I am still wearing

[139]

my ripped and bloodied English ensemble and am grateful for the change of clothes.

I arrive in the dining room just as the Queen's Guard closes the huge banquet doors and see a look of relief spread across Marist's face, a look of pure anger spread across Vassar's, and a look of disapproval from the queen. Molly has taken her seat at the far end of the table - opposite the queen. Isn't that a position reserved for special guests? Maybe this special guest is royalty, a heroic Siv, or maybe the only remaining free Alpha Spike left on the planet? Take your pick but it should not be Molly. The only reason I don't say anything is because my seat is right next to Marist's. The 100-foot long table is larger than anything I have seen before, yet, each of us are within a foot radius of each other. *English people are crazy.* The queen makes a toast and Molly responds with a raised glass.

"So, you made it to dinner, Colman, how nice," Vassar spits.

"Thank you, Vassar. I appreciate the congratulations."

"That was sarcastic. You would think that you would be a master of recognizing those types of things at this point in your life."

"I know. That was sarcasm as well. However, I would not expect you to recognize that as you already receive everything you want."

"He should have taken you out like I said," Vassar mumbles.

"What?" I say.

"Just eat your dinner," she smirks.

I look at Marist. Something flickers under her eyes that looks a bit like desire, a bit like defiance. Whatever it is, it is certainly sexy. Dinner provides a perfect atmosphere to wash away someone's artificially constructed Image. Vassar has immersed herself as always in her Profile, so it is basically Marist and I remaining at the table. Yes, there is an entire Press and camera crew waiting in the corner, but they are shooting B-roll for tonight and they are not going to be under the table, are they? I inch slightly closer to Marist.

"Colman, what are you doing? Stop," she whispers.

"I wanted to thank you for finally showing me some truth today during our outing," I say. "You are going to have to explain to me how you got this way."

"That is not a conversation for dinner."

"Then when would you like to have that conversation?"

"When there are not a million cameras around me, and I can give you more of a truthful answer."

"I know what we could do. Let me touch you and we could listen in on the conversation that Molly is having with your grandmother."

"How would we even do that?"

"Take my hand and find out."

"If this is just a ploy to…" she starts to say but I reach under the table and grab her hand. I feel my energy instantaneously start to sap away from me as I maintain the pathway. I learned how to do this trick

[141]

when I first learned to talk to female Sivs. I realized that I could transmit my state of being to another physical form and in that moment, or moments, I can completely overpower them. What Marist is experiencing is the heightened physical attributes that I have. I have not figured out a way to reverse this pathway to experience what they are feeling, but there is no need anyway. Since I can't feel emotion, it wouldn't translate.

Marist's eyes are completely dilated, and her pupils take up the entire sclera making her look like she is possessed. Double checking that the cameras are not monitoring us, I let the games begin. I hone into my hearing capabilities and reach out to both the queen and Molly from where I am sitting. This takes even more concentration because I have to translate and then supply the sound waves to Marist. It will give Marist and me something to do and will allow us an opportunity to partake in a process called 'bonding'. I search for Molly's vocal patterns in the dining room and lock onto the ones containing her pitch. Then, I reach out to the queen and lock onto hers. It is difficult to sort through the mess to find a common speech pattern and dialogue because the queen's signal is being emitted to Molly through a type of Communication software and Molly's is functioning in the same way in return.

"It is just not rational, Your Majesty. He will not go down without a fight," Molly says.

"You are quite right," the queen responds, "but you forget who makes the rules in this country."

"Your Majesty, I meant no disrespect. It's just - allowing you to do anything to him while he is abroad would greatly damage and change the way Sivs around the world view Spikes. It will affect my standing within the Country. I will not sacrifice that just to appease you."

"Watch your tone. I am not someone who would offer up nothing in return for this great sacrifice. I would be willing to offer you a position within my administration for the remainder of your life. You would not be able to return to the Country, but you could start a new life in England after it is over."

"That is a very kind offer, Your Majesty, but I will not be accepting. I have great upward mobility within the Country. I hope to one day design Spikes as a Keeper. It has been a lifelong goal of mine."

"Molly, I am not someone that Beings say no to. There is a very good reason for this. Please take tonight to reconsider your answer and if it changes, please tell me in the morning. The Guineas Stakes will take place as planned, regardless of your answer, so if you don't change your mind, that will be the last event we'll invite you to attend in England."

"Thank you, Your Majesty. We are going to be leaving tomorrow anyway," Molly says.

At that, I disconnect. I guess we're still leaving early, then. There are too many assumptions to be made from this brief conversation and if I do not ask Molly explicitly, I know she will not tell me. I look over to Marist and see that she looks worried. Does she know what they were referring to? Is the queen planning an elaborate Encounter? I would have to prepare for that. That would be an incredible payday if she is and the Country would be happy with me if I'd got another State to partake in the Pit.

"Colman, I think you should have your security detail stay on tonight. I am going to order some of my men to also guard your door. It is against regulations for Queen's Guard to attack one another so, in case my grandmother takes a cheap shot and tries to Execute you, the Guards would not even be able to get in the room," Marist says.

My SQUAD picks up on the fact that Marist and I are talking, and they have started creeping closer to the table with their boom mics and their other assortment of listening devices. I remove my hand from Marist's, and I bring it up to eat when a piece of flesh drops onto my plate. A reddened handprint is scorched into my skin. Blood has started seeping through the decayed parts of my fingers, burned almost to the bone, and as Marist catches me looking at it, she screeches and pushes away from the table so fast that the back of her chair catches and it tips backward. I am able to catch her with my good hand before she hits the ground.

Vassar doesn't bat an eye, but the queen pushes back from the head and orders her guards to attend to her granddaughter. Molly is standing and looks afraid. I already know what she is thinking. *If I have one more incident of alleged abuse toward the princess, I am going to lose all female ratings on my Profile.*

Dinner is now over. Marist is escorted away from me and does not have the chance to look back. How did I burn my hand? Did I somehow burn her hand as well?

I did not touch my plate and now I will have to get one of the cooks to make me something before I retire for the evening … alone. How have I not had physical contact in three days? This is one of the worst dry spells I have had in years. I have either been rented out or had the pleasure of picking someone to sleep with since my Entrance Day and now in England, where some of the most beautiful women live, I have not slept with a single one. Molly comes hustling over and confirms that I am no longer welcome at the table. I wonder what the queen is going to say about this.

I need an Encounter to restore my stable footing. I am taken from the dining room and returned to my wing. Molly follows me in.

"Let us be honest with each other for a moment, shall we?" Molly spits.

"I assume that honest dialogue is always what we engage in. Am I wrong?" I ask

"Cut it out, Colman, I'm not in the mood."

"Fine," I say. "What's up?"

"We need to talk about your impolite intrusion into my conversation with the queen."

She proves it. Right then, right there, she proves that Khan was not lying. I am a living machine.

[145]

There is no way she could have known I listened into her conversation because my EYE is just that advanced. She has access to my EYE. She is in control of me.

"Then let's talk about it. Which part do you want to talk about first?" I say.

"I do not know how much you heard but I am not going to be putting you in a position where there is no hope that you will live. Your Execution Day is not anytime soon. I also hope you heard that I will not be leaving you for any position she could offer me."

"So, she was trying to Execute me?"

"In a way, yes."

"What does that mean?"

"I cannot tell you what that means but I am telling you it is not going to happen tomorrow if I have any say over it. Understand?"

"Yes ma'am," I say.

"If you ever invade on a private conversation again, I will personally Execute you," she says smiling.

"Is that in your job description?"

"No but I am sure I can get clearance to add that in there."

"I think I this would be an adequate time to remind you though that I am technically your boss," I pipe up.

"Shut up, this conversation is over," she says as she looks down at the agenda for tomorrow. "As you are aware, I've decided that tomorrow will be our last day in England..."

"I am," I interject but she does not break her stride.

"And tomorrow we are going to be seeing the horses at Ascot. They have picked a special guest to ride one of the horses out for this ancient tradition. You."

"I have not ridden a horse in five years…"

"You will remember," she says confidently.

"Ok so I will be riding one out and then what? Watch the remainder of it?"

"Not quite."

"What is that supposed to mean?"

"The queen is mandating that you then compete in a race of your own afterward. The Country allows one request for the entire trip and this is what she wants to use it on. I agree with her; this will show that you are sympathetic to animals but have control over them." She pauses. "So, the last order of business today is about Marist."

"I am listening," I say.

"I need you to turn off your EYE," she says as she turns off her software. "Marist needs to be taken care of, if you know what I mean."

"In what context are we talking?" I say beginning to grin.

"She needs to be Executed," Molly says seriously.

My smile falters and then disappears. I get cotton mouth and my scorched hand begins to bleed as my blood pressure skyrockets. *Did I hear that correctly?*

"Molly, do you know how illegal that is?" I say trying to form my words.

"I do not care. Your ratings are fluctuating between one and two points. That is low for us and the Keepers are telling me that you need a boost before you come back to the Country."

"That is not going to happen."

"Why not?" she quizzically asks me. "You have never had a problem taking an Execution order before."

"No, but I cannot do that. There are regulations to be honored and I am sure there are Peace Treaties to be respected … and a whole slew of other things."

"What is really going on here?" she says and even though she tries to hide it, she is starting to get nervous. She examines my face, looking for a non-verbal answer, then her eyes linger – one second too long – when they fall on my neck. She must know at least something about the bathroom experience. Small beads of sweat are forming on her forehead and although my EYE is off, I can tell her heart rate is increasing because her carotid artery is jumping out of her neck.

"What do you mean?" I say.

"I mean - why are you disobeying an order for an Execution? You have never once done that. Did she do something to you, Colman? You need to tell me right now if something happened that was not supposed to."

"Molly, I am your boss and this conversation is boring me. It is over." There must be something about the way I say this because I am impressed by the conviction that I display. That alarms her even more because at that moment she grabs a syringe out of her jacket pocket and lunges at me, aiming for my neck. I steadily avoid her and throw her against the bed. I hear the frame crack as she connects with the wood beam.

"What are you doing?" I almost scream.

I see her on the floor studying me. I am good at reading reactions but there are too many emotions that flicker across her face. Fear, guilt, interest, dread, hope, and disgust all make a very prominent appearance. She opens her mouth and then closes it, opens it again then looks at the floor. She gets up and I prepare myself for another go but she does not make a move.

"You may have the final say when it comes to Executing people, but you've never turned me down before. I received your request to have security on duty tonight as well as a request from Marist adding her own guards outside your door. Colman, you know I will find out eventually if something goes on here. Goodnight."

She spins on her heel and she turns on her Communications software as she walks out the door.

There are so many unanswered questions.

CHAPTER 15

I wake up gasping for air as Molly opens the Tube's door, dressed in her horse racing outfit: a golden Stella McCartney dress with a hat that has dead butterflies pasted on the brim. Before anything else, I notice how exhausted my security detail seems to be. As Marist suggested I had them stay up all night with members of the Queen's Guard to watch over me. They are practically holding onto the walls for support. *I may have asked too much.*

"Were there any attempts to get into the room last night?" I ask Rosen as Molly tidies up the room, placing a plain metal box underneath the control center for the Tube.

"No, sir," they say averting their eyes. *They must be tired.*

"Just know that I hold you all in the highest esteem. You can have the day off to catch up on some rest," I say addressing my own detail first and the Queen's Guard second. "I am sure Marist will treat you the same. Thank you again."

The smallest of smiles form on my team members' lips and they nod indicating they are grateful for the reprieve. But as expected, Molly is energized and still buzzing around the room.

"Should I be prepared to put you on your ass again this morning or have you learned to control yourself?" I say.

"Uh, please, you do not know what this job entails. I reacted poorly to the stress you put me under on a daily basis. That kind of reaction should have been more warmly received. Nevertheless, I am ready to have an absolutely incredible day at the racetrack. There are going to be so many other Famous Beings there today and you are going to be in the limelight!" she squeals.

This is certainly a quick turnaround from last night.

"Are Bella and Roberto going to be coming in this morning to dress me?"

"They have already flown back but they instructed me with their job," she says swinging a large black bag which presumably contains my clothes. Her eyes linger a millisecond too long on my neck – *again* – and then she looks down at my hands.

"Why is your hand not healed?" she says quietly.

"I must not have hooked myself up appropriately last night. Don't worry, I won't show it to anyone," I say.

She tosses me the black bag and when I peer inside, I am greeted with so much color that my eyes hurt. The first item is a specially designed pair of lime-green Oscar de la Renta pants; next is a satin striped John Galliano button-down and a Tom Ford navy blue

[151]

jacket. I follow that up with a Vineyard Vines fedora and a necktie. *I am a walking rainbow.*

Molly has begun rattling off a few of the race-day traditions and a summary of the other Famous Beings who the queen said would be in attendance. Once dressed, I am ushered out of the room for the final part of my stay. I say goodbye to Buckingham Palace, strolling through the hallway until I see Vassar and the queen waiting.

"Molly, where…" I begin to say, noticing the absence of one incredibly gorgeous princess.

"Don't start. Marist will not be accompanying us today. She fell … ill last night," she says. The acid dripping from the last three words clearly expresses her disdain for this unexpected absence. *She doesn't believe it.* "I was told that if she feels better, she will join us after the race."

On our way out to the cars, the amount of ornate dresswear astounds me. Vassar is carrying a stuffed Lynx for Spike sake! But I am forced back into seclusion and as the Queen's Guard directs me towards a vehicle of my own, a hunger forms in my stomach. My detail for today looks a little shifty but it is nothing I have not dealt with before. Molly estimated the trip to take 1 hour 26 minutes, so I better do something to occupy my time. I scoot up to the front of the car and tap on the black windowpane separating the driver and me. The window rolls down and I ask him to put on some music to ease my mind.

A pressure has formed behind my eyes and my temples throb with the blood pounding in my head. Bringing my hand up to my face to massage my temples, something hot drips onto my nose. My hand is still charred from yesterday and blood has resurfaced under the skin. This is why I must check all the IVs before I am sent to sleep.

I page Molly over our Communication software and she picks up immediately. *Odd.*

"Yes?" she sighs nervously. She always sighs when something is on her mind.

"Is everything ok?" I respond.

"Why wouldn't it be?"

"Something is seriously wrong with my hand. Even without the IV last night, I should be healed by now."

"How did you burn your hand?" she asks slowly. She must know how it happened, but I will not give her the satisfaction.

"It must have been yesterday during Khan's interrogation."

"Interesting. Well, it should have already healed. There is nothing I can do about it now."

I'm confused by her tone. She's always hyper-concerned about my well-being. "Should I be concerned? This is the first time this has happened."

"I will take care of it at the racetrack." She is trying to sound cheerful.

"Molly, what is going on?"

"Nothing is going on. Look, I have a lot on my plate trying to get endorsements and ratings as well as to repair your Image. If there isn't anything else, I need to go."

"Since when am I your second priority? Who else in your life is more important than me?"

"Just know that I am doing this for you," she says cautiously.

Three seconds later, my EYE lights up with a notification from Fanto. *Shouldn't they be asleep?* I answer it.

"This is against regulation, but we agreed that we should tell you," she blurts out.

That is never a good sign.

"There was a disturbance last night. Molly came back in after she initially left. She injected something into your healing reserves."

I pause, unsure of whether this is a test or not. "Do you know what it was?"

"No, but we were told not to say anything to you. We overheard your fight last night and although her job is to protect you, we think that something is wrong. She came into the room last night and said that there was a scheduled upgrade to your sleeping chambers, but she didn't do anything to the Tube itself. Instead, she injected something into the reserves."

"Thank you, Fanto. Please tell the rest of the team that I appreciate the honesty. I will not mention this to anybody else and I suggest you do the same."

"Yes, sir. Thank you, sir. See you on the tarmac after your race."

I end the conversation, lean back into the cushioned seat of the Rolls and close my eyes trying to assess the situation. Molly being weird and aloof is out of the ordinary. Why would she make an adjustment to my Tube without telling me? Does this explain why my hand is fluctuating between a deep red and a light pink? Did she inject something into the system that is not going to let me heal as quickly? *But why would she do that?* My blood concentration is close to 100% so it makes no sense why every aspect of my body is not functioning correctly. What could she have put in the Tube? It must have been some type of platelet thinning agent. That is the only way the blood in my hand would stop clotting. I am built to reject every common form of medicine and foreign agent so whatever she put in there was specifically designed for my genotype.

I close my eyes, hoping to pass the time and the minute I do, I start dreaming. Marist, Molly, Fanto, Downey, Cassidy, Vassar, Rosen, Bella, the queen, Kendall Khan, Roberto, and two other individuals I cannot identify form before me, and it is as if I am inside and outside of the car at the same time. I have closed my eyes, but I am still completely conscious. Soon I am in an Embassy with everyone around me, and I am strapped to a board. All my limbs are restrained.

Khan is making his way towards me with something that looks like a mace, as the rest of the audience makes a circle around me, staring at me. He stops right in front of me, brings the mace up and over his head, and brings it down right toward me. My physical projection closes its eyes, but I am not associated with the figure. Khan uses the downward momentum and instead of Executing me, he lets the mace fly right toward Rosen.

The mace impales his face and his body collapses. My projection has his eyes open now and is screaming. Water is streaming down his face and he is shaking his head. He mouths something but Khan picks up the mace and proceeds to bash in the heads of my whole team. Fanto is Executed, Cassidy is Executed, Downey is Executed. My projection is straining against the board with water still flowing down his face. Are those tears? I have not seen them before but have read about them. Tears happen when Sivs get really sad and cannot function properly. It should be impossible for my personal projection to form tears.

Khan taps all the Executed beings and, like smoke, they disappear one by one. Khan takes Vassar and removes her from the group, and she goes to stand behind him. Marist looks at her sister and starts to point at her, but Khan has acquired some kind of sword and severs her arm with one swoop. Blood starts to pour out of her limb, and she clutches it in pain as she collapses on the floor. He takes the sword, raises it, and then brings it down on her head. She is Executed.

My projection has stopped crying and now looks 'angry'. Anger occurs when something does not go your way and you cannot rationalize it. The restraints are pulled taught against my body as the projection continues to pull against the board. Bella and Roberto surge forward to cradle Marist but Khan has a flame-thrower and is burning them alive. Their bodies are shuddering on the ground as they hold on to each other, do they kiss? I always imagined Bella and Roberto as a good couple. Khan moves toward Molly next, but my projection starts pleading with him.

"No, Kendall, please, I will do anything. Please, please do not do that to her. Execute me instead."

Khan does not take any heed and proceeds to shoot Molly in the chest with a gun. *What?* Guns are not allowed in the Pit. She clutches her chest, trying to suck in air but I can already tell that it is not going to do her any good. My projection has resorted back to yelling as he shakes his body against the restraints. Molly is looking at me and she says she is proud of me. Why does she say that?

Khan moves toward the queen next. She holds up her hands like she is apologizing but he does not accept it. She turns to run but he appears on the other side of her. He has acquired barb wire and is stringing it around her neck. She starts yelling but, other than the two people I don't know left in the room, no one but Khan and myself can hear her. Khan gives a sharp tug on the wire and it cuts into her neck. She turns but the wire digs itself in further and she is leaking blood all over her robes. She collapses on the floor and he kicks her. My projection looks numb on the board. He has his head lowered. He is no longer crying and screaming. He looks like an uninhabited Being. Nothing is emerging from his mouth. There are now only four people left in the Embassy. The two random people move forward and stand in the way of my projection as Khan advances toward me. He stops and smiles.

"There is no reason you cannot come out of here alive. I will forgive this demonstration if you step away now. You could create another one."

The two unknown people are impassive, and his smile gets bigger. I see my projection looks towards these people with absolute disbelief. Why would strangers give their life for me? Khan pulls out three gas masks. One he puts on, one he gives to Vassar, and one he hands to the random female to put on me. After she is done attaching the mask to my face, she steps back into formation with the male. Khan shouts something and the room is filled with a gas. It comes swirling in. Milky white and silent, this gas does not seem like something that would cause any harm. In fact, it looks like it would comfort you.

But the people standing in front of me start to twitch. Their bodies convulse and they fall, holding each other, to the floor. By some miracle, both manage to turn their bodies around and look at me as they die. Khan erupts into a fit of laughter as he takes off his gas mask. He is obviously very happy with the outcome. Something registers in my projection's face, but I lose my point of view before I can identify what it was.

Vassar leaves the room, hanging her head out of fear, as Khan advances towards my projection strapped to the board. He chops the people on the floor up with the sword he used on Marist as he moves forward. They are now in pieces all around me. He takes the final step closer to my projection and whispers something in his ear. I try to rush forward, to get closer to my projection, but there is something holding me back. Whatever Khan just told my projection, he does not like it and he spits at him. This outrages Khan but through brilliant white teeth he sneers, "Now it is my time to rule."

There is a swipe of a fire-hot spike and my projection's head falls off his body and onto the floor. Khan stands there looking down at the pool of blood accumulating around his feet. He looks almost shocked at what he just did. Anger and terror permeate through every pore in his body and he scans the room looking for help, until he makes eye contact from where I am watching him. He charges toward me, but the entire scene disappears…

A tapping on the window jolts me back into reality. The car has stopped. The door opens and I see the familiar flashes of cameras. *How did we get here already?* My eyes were closed for two minutes. I see Molly's head appear from the outside and she looks exhausted but manages to put on a smile for me.

"Time to get out, Colman. Ascot awaits."

I slide to the edge of the seat by the door, hear the initial gasps and screams from my fans and the smile forms on my face.

What a weird dream.

CHAPTER 16

I make my way from the car to the edge of the stables without looking at the Press, ignoring their incessant screaming of my name and rush of inane questions. This may be the first time in my life that I cannot face the flashing lightbulbs. Molly trots behind me and at one point, asks me to fix my smile. *She has never said that before – ever.* The Sivs running alongside of me as I stride into the stables to look at the horses before the race are pestering me for autographs and pictures, but I deny every one of them. The barricade to the stables is so close. But as I reach the door, a boy, about ten Siv years old, pulls on my jacket.

"Excuse me, Colman?"

"I can't sign anything right now, sorry, kid," I say.

"Do you remember me?" he says calmly.

"I'm sorry, I do not," I say and I mean it. I would remember someone like him. He has the brightest blue eyes I have ever seen.

"You Executed my family two years ago when we came to the Country," he says.

At this, this little morsel of drama, the Press surges forward throwing all their listening devices in the space between me and this young boy.

"I'm sorry for that." This conversation could be good for my ratings.

"They should not have paid to try to Execute you," he says matter-of-factly. I hear one of the reporters behind me gasp. Come on, this little boy even knows it is foolish to pay to Encounter me.

"At least you understand. Thanks for stopping by today."

"Okay," he says plainly, gazing at me with his ice-crystal eyes.

What else should I say?

As if reading my mind, he snaps, "Aren't you going to at least apologize?"

I have to apologize? For them trying to kill me? I look around for an escape. There is none.

Finally, I say, "I am sorry about your family, but it was nice meeting you."

I continue my path into the barn, doing my best to ignore the exchange. Surely, Molly set that up. The Press is visibly shocked as I walk away and not one of them follows me in. The pressure from the car ride has returned and I turn around to watch the little boy being carried off by the guards. The Press is following him, attempting to get a statement from him.

The distinct and glorious smell of horses greet me as I mosey into the barn. I make my way along the stalls and look at each of the horses inside, scrolling through all the different names of horses as I go: Irish War Cry, Birch Tree Lumberjack, Smiling All the Way,

Humble, Can't Stop Me, Clancy Lowered the Boom, Australia's Finest, Dubai Baby, and Jack the Ripper.

Jack the Ripper is in the back of his stall and is an objectively majestic animal. With a name like his, one would expect a midnight black horse with a short, neat mane. This horse, on the other hand, is the purest shade of white. There is not a single black, grey, or brown hair anywhere on his body and he shimmers when he moves. All the other horses are neighing or moving but this horse is standing completely still. *Is he fake?* My EYE detects a pulse.

Moving closer towards the stall, the horse takes one step towards me as I open the door. I take a step into the immaculate stall and as if I am real royalty, one of his front legs trembles and slowly bends to let his head down. *Is this animal bowing to me?* What animal is able to bow?

In a moment of uncertainty, I reach out to touch the horse, but he rears back, kicking his front two legs out in front of him. He catapults me into the closed door, and I crumple into a pile of hay. Molly comes rushing forward asking if I am hurt, and then starts cursing the horse for ruining my Image. I shake her off and start laughing. This horse does not like being touched. I tell Molly that this is the horse I want to ride. *I will conquer it.*

"Colman. I know you are confident in your riding ability and you are excited, but this horse does not want to be ridden. The jockey even said he is nervous to get on him."

"I have a feeling that I will be able to make it work."

"Why don't you try Birch Tree Lumberjack? He is the favorite for today's races."

"I want this horse. I think that was a good omen."

"A good omen. A good omen to you is being kicked through a stall and breaking your ribs?"

"Yes, actually, it is today."

"Very well, but when it doesn't go smoothly don't come crawling back to me."

"Don't worry, I never learned to crawl. I come out fighting."

She smiles and I go back towards the horse and attempt to bow again. But before I do, the horse bows again. Strange. This time, instead of going towards the horse I let him approach me. I bow and hold my posture until I feel his breath on my neck. I slowly stand up and he begins to back away, so I fold myself back over and hold the position. Again, he gets close enough so that I feel his breath on my neck but this time I do not stand. I hold the bow until his nostrils have touched from the tips of my head and across both shoulders. After he is done smelling, I slowly rise, and he looks like he is waiting for something to happen.

Fully upright, Jack turns his body sideways and I begin to inch closer to him. This time he doesn't seem to mind. I plant one hand gently on his side expecting him to move away but he doesn't. Sliding my hand over his hair, moving up toward his mane, he stands completely still but also seems completely relaxed. My head is directly opposite his and my arms are on either side of his neck. It probably looks like I am making a move on this horse.

He draws his head up toward me and the initial eye contact makes me feel weird. His eyes capture mine and I imagine that he can see right through me. I rest my forehead against his head and for the first time in a long time, my entire mind goes blank. I do not know how my body kept standing but I totally lose myself. Molly comes back around and pulls me out of the trance saying I must get out of the stable so the jockey can tack up the horse. I look into Jack's eyes a final time and then leave, feeling even weirder than I did before.

Molly asks me to hold a brief press conference and I oblige knowing that I have certainly disobeyed her wishes in the past 24 hours. The Press is already assembled making me think back to Khan's comments from my interrogation. *She knew I would say yes before she even asked me.* I mount the podium and the Press lets me have it.

"Colman, there are rumors that princess Marist is pregnant with your child. How did this happen?"

"Let me ask you a question in return. It's really simple, I promise. Your brain can handle it, I am sure. Did you think that through before you asked me?"

"Yes," she states uncertainly.

[165]

"Wrong. Alpha Spikes cannot have children and we are not allowed to have a family. Make sure the next question is better, ok?"

She blushes. "Thank you…"

"Sure. Next?" I spit.

"Colman, there is the belief that you are now a prude. Is that true?"

"A prude? Because I have not had sex in three days? Although that is a slightly better question, it is also not true. If you want, you can go back into your archives and see my last tape with the Duchess from Austria. Thanks. Next?"

"What happened to Princess Marist today?"

"I don't know what happened to her today," I say honestly. "I was briefed as I walked out towards the cars this morning that she is ill and will not be joining us."

"Does it have anything to do with the harm you inflicted upon her in the bathroom of the Globe?"

"Those rumors are patently untrue," I say quickly. "I did not cause any harm to the princess."

"Then what happened to the stalls? We all saw pictures and it did not look like you were simply helping her clean up her dress."

"What I was doing in the bathroom is classified. That is for myself and my team to know."

"Did you have an Encounter? Were there Sivs in there waiting to ambush you?"

"Again, I cannot comment. That is for my team and my team only. Next question please."

"Who was that child who approached you today as you were entering the barn?"

"And we are done!" Molly interrupts, pushing me away from the microphone. "Thank you, guys, you are dismissed."

Something is definitely wrong. Those are the types of questions that catalyze major rating increases; she should have let me answer it. I would have been able to spin it precisely how she wanted it. She picks up her agenda from behind the podium and does not look at me as she informs me that Jack the Ripper is ready for me.

Sure enough, Jack is ready to ride and looks like a freaking beast when he is tacked up. His jockey is not so excited to hand me the reins, but I ease his mind by saying that I do this all the time. I feel pure power beneath me when I mount the animal; it is like feeling the engine beneath a Koenigsegg CCXR Trevita. I slowly let go of the reins and Jack responds immediately by walking forward. I give the slightest pull back and he stops. He answers to the smallest command. I wonder if he is controlled by a computer too.

The other horses are starting to file out and Jack joins them. He is the last to file in and the huge crowd in the grandstands screams when we walk out. There are Sivs dressed in their best, waiting to see if they are going to take home some extra money today and I get a shot of adrenaline just seeing their reaction. Jack is steady beneath me and I already feel like I do

[167]

not want to get off him. I feel physically confident in this animal. How much would he sell for? No, I wouldn't do that. I do not have any dwelling to keep him near the city and a horse like this deserves to be raced as long as he can.

We move into the pre-race paddock and I am told to bring him onto the track to run him in front of the Sivs. I am used to being in front of all these Beings, but my heart momentarily races with the thought of running Jack without knowing what he is like. I make the educated decision that I can handle it and steer him towards the opening of the track. We get on and I feel something change beneath me. No longer is he calm and relaxed - now he is anxious. He surges forward and I pull back on the reins and pat his shoulder.

"There we go, kid. You got this. It's one gallop down and one gallop back. That's it and then I'll turn you back over to your jockey," I say to him.

"Ladies and gentlemen. Sivs of all ages…" The announcer's voice bellows over the loudspeakers. "Put your hands together to welcome the royal family's special guest, Mr. Colman Cai."

The smile mounts my face and I let go of the reins and Jack moves forward. He walks, that walk turns into a trot and that trot turns into a full-blown gallop. There are thousands of people watching right now but I forget about every single one of them. I am racing on a physically attractive and unusually intelligent thoroughbred at Ascot. This is what they must mean when they say, 'Life does not get better than this'. I am speeding along the track at 45MPH, the wind whipping alongside me with a fresh stretch of dirt before me. Knowing I must slow down soon, I pull back on the reins in order to stop Jack and turn him around. He does as instructed.

He spins around and my body is thrown to the right side of the saddle as something impales me in my shoulder. I start sliding off but grip the reins to keep my balance. Something is very wrong. I glance towards my shoulder and see an arrow protruding from it in a bloody rush.

"What the..." I begin to say but Molly's voice drowns me out.

"Colman get off the track!" she screeches through my Communication platform.

I start to gallop again as another arrow misses my head by less than an inch.

"You need to get out of the inner track right now!" she screams more desperately than I have ever heard before.

Jack the Ripper is running more quickly but not quick enough. My EYE is fully functioning, and it detects two more arrows coming at me. The first one misses my torso but the second strikes me right below the first one. I try to move the fingers in my left arm, but it is completely paralyzed.

"Colman, the queen is going to try to Execute you. Stop! You need to..." Molly says but our connection is interrupted by static.

[169]

The Communication cuts off from Molly's side and, in my confusion while trying to reconnect, I lose grip on the reins and fall off of Jack. I hit the ground with a hard thud and momentarily see stars. I sit up just in time to move out of the trajectory of an arrow flying my way as Jack gallops out of my view. I dodge this arrow and try to ascertain where the arrows are coming from. Across the rooftop of the stands are archers with huge crossbows. Each of them is notching an arrow, aiming at me. What I thought were thousands of Sivs in the stands were only holograms and many of them are blinking out of existence as more arrows come my way. The barn doors are shut so my exit is compromised. The scene I witnessed just a minute earlier – full of life – now alludes to my Execution.

I want to taunt the archers and show them how fast I can run but my arm will not be able to pump and therefore I will not be able to carry momentum. Suddenly, a baying sound rips through the air from the outer track and I swivel to see a dozen dogs sprinting around the bend. My EYE zooms in on them and I can see there is foam flying from their mouths as the outline of five monster horses gallop behind him. The dogs stand five feet tall at their shoulder and are genetically altered. They have massive, muscular bodies and are sprinting around 20 MPH. Behind them are five huge horses, definitely not meant for racing. They each carry one gigantic Siv, each armed with crossbows. *At least the queen did not cheat and arm them with guns*. That is a positive right? It looks like England is pulling out all the stops to give me the most authentic experience possible. I get to see a horse race and a fox hunt all in one day!

CHAPTER 17

After compiling my options and performing an analysis on the situation, I conclude that I can do one of two things: run, to have more time to assess the situation, or face them. Since there are far too many of them, I pick the first option. Ripping the two arrows out of my body, as a torrent of blood starts coating my paralyzed arm, I know that I have twenty minutes before I die from blood loss. Sending a Repair code from my EYE, hoping that it can temporarily act as my primary motor cortex until this Encounter is over, my rock bottom is approaching more quickly than ever before. This type of manual override is used as a last resort because if the EYE acts as an artificial pathway between the arm and brain for too long, it establishes a permanent pathway and I could lose movement forever. As much as Khan wants me to believe that I am a robot, I am not going to give him that satisfaction.

My EYE blinds me as it creates the artificial pathway and then I feel a sensation in my arm. I flex my fingers and it works – the pathway is a success. With a timer on for ten minutes – anything longer than ten minutes will sever that natural pathway for good – I start running. The dogs are getting closer as the horses snort behind them. Halfway around the bend, My Way by Frank Sinatra comes blaring through the speakers of the track and I laugh to myself because I respect the queen's humor. During seriously violent Encounters, I become genuinely happy. *Must be the assassin in me.*

This is what I was created to do. I am reaching a higher purpose in my life during these moments. My vision clears, my respiration rate stabilizes, my EYE launches into overdrive and my brain clears itself of nonessential information. It is like falling into a lake at night. The water is dark and cold, and you cannot orient yourself but when you finally come back to the surface you are alive. I have made it a quarter of the way around the track when the first symptoms of blood loss begin to work their way through my body. I cannot do this forever and ten minutes may have been a generous estimate. I cannot ask for many other functions from my EYE, so I need to find a weapon the old-fashioned way – by myself.

The archers send another volley of arrows down at me as I race down the back of the track. One arrow impales itself in my quadricep and I quickly pull it out

[Alert. Blood Analysis. Blood Concentration: 83%. Decreasing.]

The tip is covered in blood and I stare at my liquid-life thinking of how few times I have encountered a situation like this. The blood is already drying on the jagged top. That's when it hits me - an idea, not another arrow. These arrows may function as a way to Execute me, but they can also Execute the things chasing me. After all, these arrows are provided to me courtesy of the queen, it would be churlish not to use them...

The dogs are gaining on me as I continue running down the back, and the queen's voice booms out of the speakers: "Young spike, it has been my absolute pleasure to watch you these past few days. I have followed your movements and Executions from the time you were created, and I must say you never cease to amaze me. But your time has come to leave this cruel world you were born into. You have no one to save you and I apologize that I am the one that has to do this. I have grounded your security and Molly is being held in your car. In the event that you die, she will be allowed to return to the Country. She is a lovely girl, but I cannot have her getting in my way."

"This is not my day, you crazy old lady!" I yell breathlessly towards the center stands. She obviously does not hear me.

"Now onto the fun part! The dogs behind you have been genetically engineered in a lab with canine DNA and electronic parts, just like you were, so you can imagine what bloodlust they must have. The Sivs on top of the horses are the prototypes of England's very own Spike Program. Oh, the best part! Once you are Executed, we are going to retrieve your body to study your physiological and chemical makeup to make the best Spikes in the world. Best of luck."

That was not a very good monologue for a final farewell. Quite frankly, I expected it to be more elegant. Now back at the starting line, more arrows come arching my way as the dogs break through the hedges separating the inner track from the outer track. They make a direct path towards me and although I cannot see or hear the horses, I know that they cannot jump the hedges because their bodies are too massive. *Time to take care of the freaky mutts.*

Three arrows in my hand, I glance at the pack of twelve dogs behind me and unless I can collect more arrows on the next lap, one arrow per four dogs has to be the rule. The lead dog breaks from the pack and barrels through the hedges of the inner track while continuing to follow my trajectory. I cannot see it, but I can hear it. Honed into its breathing, I sense it coming closer until we lock speeds. Three seconds later, it leaps back through the hedges into the outer track, its snarling muzzle aimed for my face.

Taking one of the arrows, I pierce its skin and break through the skull, but sparks fly at me as I do so. There is a computer chip encased in the part of the skull where the frontal lobe should be. I have to keep running in order to avoid the rest of the pack, but I cannot let this thing revive. I reach through the skull and rip the computer chip from its casing and the dog falls still.

[Encounter: Target Executed. Targets Remaining: Sixteen: 11 Canine, 5 Robot.]

As I disconnect the computer chip from the main body, there is a resounding howl and I am alerted to the location of the rest of the pack. They are way too close and two more dogs bolt through the hedges behind me. Sprinting in the other direction, a stroke of

[175]

genius bites me like the oncoming pack. Perhaps the pack is a closed circuit?

I crush the chip in my hand and from different parts of the track, I hear mechanical whines from the remaining members. The dogs behind me slow fractionally. The first dog was one-twelfth of the energy, so I need to destroy three more dogs to make a difference. The two behind me are still on my path and the tail of a mutt in the bushes up ahead alerts me that an ambush is nearing. I guess it is time to face the two behind me and I slow down and reverse direction.

The mutts leap on me in an instant. The razor-sharp teeth tear through my already injured shoulder as I bring an arrow up into the belly of one of them, pulling down to expose the circuitry under the fake fur. With the inner workings exposed, I expect it to stop but no such luck. *Damn, they can only be stopped through the brain.* Reaching up, I grab the first dog's neck and twist. I send an arrow through the head and reach in to grab the computer chip. Out it pops and I crush it in my hand as I pull the third dog into a headlock.

[Encounter: Target Executed. Targets Remaining: Eleven: 9 Canine, 5 Robot.]

Around the bend, where the other dogs were waiting, another whine gives up their sneaky position. The mutts are moving five miles slower than they were before but up ahead, two of the horsemen make themselves visible followed by a pack of four dogs. The horses are galloping toward me at probably 30 MPH so

I reverse direction once again, but the blood loss is affecting my speed.

The barking mutts from behind the horsemen have gotten quieter but they should not be my focus now, I will have to take on the two horsemen if I want to live. As I run, another volley fires toward me and I subconsciously glance at the timer. I am five minutes down before I will have to give up my left arm again. The archers on the roof are shooting exactly every two and a half minutes. The first volley was at 2 minutes 30 seconds and now at five minutes, the arrows are flying again. Setting the second timer on my EYE, I will be forced make this work in my favor.

The horsemen are gaining but I pluck two more arrows from the ground as I run. The horses are huge, probably ten or eleven feet high, and the beasts on their back look less than welcoming. I must act. I do not know what these English Spikes are made of but hopefully these Spikes are partial robots like the dogs. Leaping up onto the side rail of the track, I start running on it as the horses near. Fifteen feet, then ten feet, and the horsemen take their crossbows off their back and notch arrows when the horse's head is within an arm's length.

As I jump down on to the inner track, the horseman lets his first arrow fly. His discharge spooks the other horse and the one on the left loses control. The horses collide and the horseman loses balance, falling off the horse. I make a quick change of direction and run towards the fallen giant; he is disoriented but anticipates my move. He starts to stand but I throw myself at him and knock him back to the ground before he can stand upright. Rolling around on the ground, in what I would call a loving embrace, I am trying to get my arrows toward his throat as he tries to use his thumbs to pop my eyes. Is this what Love feels like?

We stop rolling and my years of experience come in handy. Lifting my legs, I wrap them around his head and hoist myself on his shoulders. From up here, I see how clumsy this male is. I take one of my arrows and use the razor's edge to slit his throat. He falls to his knees, but the other horseman is coming to his aid. Using a saw-like motion, I detach his head from his body and from the gaping hole starts spewing a combination of oil and gas.

[Encounter: Target Executed. Targets Remaining: Thirteen: 9 Canine, 4 Robot.]

I jump off the severed body and pick up the fallen Spike's crossbow. *This is going to be a good time.* I bet Queeny did not expect this when she played her cards. I notch an arrow in the bow, pull it back, and send it straight into the rider's chest where it reflects off the metal chest plate. The sparks startle the horse because soon the horse is rearing back, throwing the man who then lands straight onto one of the mutts.

[Encounter: Target Executed. Targets Remaining: Twelve: 8 Canine, 4 Robot.]

The horse bolts away but the pseudo-Spike regains composure and strides toward me as I close on him. I did not anticipate that his crossbow would be notched, and an arrow strikes my already-destroyed left arm. The artificial pathway is still functioning, so I keep going. *One minute until the next round of volleys.* I need to time this precisely. Leaving the arrow lodged in my arm, I load my own arrow into my stolen crossbow. It misses but the Spike stupidly follows its trajectory and looks over his shoulder where it strikes the ground. A word for the wise, do not take your eyes off a target.

Dropping the crossbow, I leap towards his face as he turns back towards me. I plunge two arrows, one in each hand, straight down into the Spike's skull as he crumples to the ground.

[Encounter: Target Executed. Targets Remaining: Eleven: 8 Canine, 3 Robot.]

Without realizing, the dogs have snuck up on me and one tears into my quad, as another attacks my arm while the final one goes to bite my neck. Before it can close its jaws, I snap the mechanical hinges underneath the furry exterior, but it continues to move. As the other two tears into the other parts of my body, I sink an arrow into the dog's skull.

[Encounter: Target Executed. Targets Remaining: Ten: 7 Canine, 3 Robot.]

The other two whine in response and, taking this opportunity, I grab both of them by the scruff of their neck and bash their heads into one another.

[Alert. Blood Analysis. Blood Concentration: 74%. Decreasing.]

Crap! I continue bashing their heads in until their skulls break from the sheer force.

[Encounter: Target Executed. Targets Remaining: Eight: 5 Canine, 3 Robot.]

I judge that there are thirty seconds until the next volley of arrows as two more horsemen come around the bend.

Standing in the middle of the track without any protection, they spur their horses into a gallop as I spring towards the final stretch of the track – directly in front of the deserted stadium with the archers on top. *Twenty seconds.* Running at 25 MPH, I feel the immense disadvantage of the blood loss again and a golf-ball sized black spot is creeping into my field of view. My vision is blurring, my breathing is laborious, but there is also a weird feeling in my stomach that is beginning to work its way up into my throat. *Ten seconds.*

Three more dogs sway around the opposite corner. I am in the middle of three murderous dogs on one end and two huge Spikes on the other; I could not be in a better position. *Eight seconds.* Confirming that I will intersect the dogs if I continue to run at this speed, the only other escape is to face the horsemen. *Five seconds.* The baying of the dogs hurts my ears as they sprint closer to their prey. *Four.* I breathe in. *Three.* I breathe out. One of the dogs jumps. I slide below it. *Two.* The archers on the roof blindly send their arrows down on me. The two remaining dogs jump at me. *One.* The first arrow impales the leaping dogs as I slide beneath their meager cover.

[Encounter: Target Executed. Targets Remaining: Five: 4 Canine, 1 Robot.]

The Spikes have fallen off their horses and the dogs are Executed in front of me. *I only have two and a half more minutes of the EYE connection.*

[Alert. Blood Analysis. Blood Concentration: 64%. Decreasing.]

"Very well, Colman," the queen says.

Seriously, what is that woman still doing here?

"I see that you have evaded me thus far. I do not think you will live to see the remainder of this day but in case you do, I want you to consider this proposal." I can hear the nerves shake in her voice. I think she has finally come to realize that I'm going to survive. She is trying to cover her ass.

"I want to offer you the chance to work for me, here, in England," she yells.

"That will never happen. You are a disloyal, hypocritical psychopath and I already have enough of those in my life," I laugh as I tune her out. *Is that the right choice?* With two minutes remaining on my left arm, I will not be able to carry my body after the pathway expires. *She can stop this right now.*

I start sprinting, determined to find the other horseman before the clock runs out, and as I turn the first corner, I am greeted by such a lovely sight. The four remaining mutts are waiting for me, but these dogs do not start running at me; they stand there, baying together as foam spills from their jaws. As I am about to strike, the last horseman ambushes me from the

[181]

hedges but overshoots most of me and his horse lands on one of the dogs in front of me.

[Encounter: Target Executed. Targets Remaining: Four: 3 Canine, 1 Robot.]

Damn, these horses are really helping me out today.

The three dogs jump at me, but I see the physical strain the closed circuit has on them. They try to run but the fastest they can move is 10 MPH now. Grabbing the arrow out of my left arm, my timer simultaneously clicks to one and a half minutes. I pull it back like I am throwing a football and let it fly at the oncoming pack. It connects with the lead dog's head and the skeleton splits in two.

[Encounter: Target Executed. Targets Remaining: Three: 2 Canine, 1 Robot.]

The horseman is able to rein in his horse but there is no way I can outrun him, so I throw myself into the hedges to avoid the hooves. One hoof hits me on my leg as I enter the green shrubbery and I try to wiggle myself out of the ensnaring branches, but the two dogs have bitten into my legs and are dragging me out backward. Feeling the skin rip off both of my calves, I'm bleeding like I've never bled before and the timer is down to a minute remaining on my fake connection.

[Alert. Blood Analysis. Blood Concentration: 51%. Decreasing.]

I try twisting out of their grips but then reverse direction when a huge shadow encapsulates my body. A crossbow is aimed right at my throat. The Spike looks at me, but I highly doubt anything is registering behind his eyes. *Did they give him a brain?*

"Colman, you have fought valiantly but you have continued to defy my wishes. I am a woman who is used to getting what she wants so I wanted to remind you who I am. My Spike is going to Execute you and there is nothing you can do about it. Both Molly and the Country will be notified. By the time the Country can retaliate, we will have already sent our vast stores of chemical weapons to Execute every last Being in your country. England will finally regain its former glory," the queen's voice bellows from her nine-foot mouthpiece.

I have Executed so many Beings over ten years and wonder if any Being has been able to find peace before they have left this world. I check my EYE one final time where 40 seconds remain on the clock. At least I can use my left hand for the remainder of my life. I close my eyes as I see the Spike put his finger on the trigger. *This is it.* Does anything come after Execution? Then a rapid-fire thudding comes from a distant area behind me. I think I am hallucinating but I open my eyes anyway. There is a blur of white that comes barreling around the corner and in less than one second, the Spike is on the ground. Jack the Ripper is trampling the dogs.

[Encounter: Target Executed. Targets Remaining: 1 Robot.]

My clock is showing 20 seconds. I grab the fallen crossbow and crawl towards the Spike. Five seconds later, I triumphantly raise it and send the first arrow into his chest. *Nine seconds*. I grab another arrow out of my body and send it into the Spike's neck. It starts to ooze a black, oily substance. I grab another arrow out of my leg and notch it and let it loose right into the skull. *Six seconds*. I go and slit the Spike's throat and watch as his head falls away from the rest of his body. *Four seconds*. I go into my EYE and send the signal to disconnect from the artificial pathway. *Three seconds*.

[Error.]

No! *Two seconds*. I send it again. *One second.*

[Terminated.]

My left arm flops against my side. Hoisting my body over Jack the Ripper, I cannot fathom why this horse came back to save me. Molly and my entire SQUAD come running through the barn as I arrive and collapse on the floor. I give Jack a kiss and he whinnies.

Goodnight world.

CHAPTER 18

I wake up in my Tube back at Buckingham Palace and I immediately pull the medical lines from my body. When it is apparent that I am safe, the swell of adrenaline leaves me with a pounding headache. How does it make any rational sense to bring me back here? The queen just tried to Execute me!

"You must hate me, Colman!" Molly says, rushing over to check me for major injuries. "Actually, wait no, you can't hate me. Never mind, it doesn't matter. I had no idea that the queen would go back on her word! This is what the conversation was about the night before. She said she would offer me a position in her administration if I made you an easy target. I assumed she meant vulnerable not actually a single stand-alone figure in the middle of a racetrack."

"Molly, how did you think it was a good idea to bring me back here?"

"Don't worry. Once I was locked in the car, I realized they did not take my Communication platforms so I immediately alerted Country Special Ops stationed in England. They came and liberated us one minute before you finished your Encounter on the track. We ran up to the control room of the racetrack, but the queen had already disappeared. That's when we saw you and there was no way for us to get to you, so we

[185]

released the horse your rode out on. We had no idea that it would react the way it did, but we were very pleased where how things turned out."

"Jack the Ripper saved me," I say, smiling.

"The horse did take out the remaining dogs and horseman, didn't he?" Molly responds.

"Why did I black out at 48%? I thought 40% was the threshold."

"We will discuss that later. The good thing is that you are physically fine now."

"Where's the queen?" I ask.

"We're not sure. but your team secured the palace after we alerted them to the problem."

"We commandeered an ancient castle from the queen?" I laugh.

"Desperate times call for desperate measures," Molly says slyly.

"Do we know where Marist is?" I ask.

"We searched the castle, sir," Rosen says. It makes me jump – I had no idea they were in here. "But we found no trace of her. Her sleeping quarters were completely vacant." He shrinks away from me. There is more to the story, more to what they found in her sleeping quarters.

"And?" I ask but the team shakes their heads. Clearly, they all agreed beforehand that they wouldn't tell me, whatever it is. Checking my EYE, I see that I am back to 100% and I feel physically more stable. Blood is an incredible substance. It can provide so

much energy when it is in you, but when it is outside …
well, that is never a good sign.

"Are we still leaving today?"

"We have to leave tomorrow. We obtained a
Country mandated order that we can stay in the palace
until tomorrow. Tonight, you can do anything you
want."

"Ok then, I say that it is time to bring out the
big guns. Molly, I am going to need a guest list of all
the Famous Beings within a hundred-mile radius of this
castle. When life gives you a palace, you throw a
party."

"No way, Bronco," Molly says, holding out
her hands. "After what happened today, we are not
inviting a bunch of strange people in here. You need to
rest."

Dammit. I need a bunch of attractive strangers
to be here. I know 100% I will end the night sleeping
with someone. *I need this English curse to end.*

She studies me. "If you need a woman for
tonight, it can be arranged."

Of course she's reading my mind. "Then
arrange it. Maybe more than one, for this
inconvenience." I wink at her.

She wrinkles her nose and leaves; security
follows her out.

I am alone in my room—which feels more like
a prison cell, now. I feel restless, desperate for
distraction. As I stand there, a slight draft tickles my
back. *A window has opened.* I initiate my EYE.

[187]

[Diagnostic Test. Begin. Heat Signature: Registered. 99 degrees Fahrenheit to NE corner.]

"I have had a long day," I say as I turn.

"I know you have had a long day. I watched it," Vassar says as she steps out of the shadows.

Great. Of all the women that could be in my room right now, does it have to be her?

"Vassar, how kind of you to set me up today. I gave quite a performance, didn't I?" I ask, analyzing her frame. She is completely unarmed.

"I knew you were going to survive. My stupid grandmother deserved to be thwarted. It is all part of the plan."

"What is that supposed to mean?"

"You will find out eventually. Anyway, I wanted to tell you that the queen is going to try to take back the palace tonight."

"You think I am actually going to believe this?" I say sarcastically.

"You don't have to. I don't care. Maybe if you don't believe me, it will be better television for everyone watching at home," she says and then she leaps back through the window as I rush forward to grab her. The night is already so dark, and my EYE cannot detect anything outside the window.

How did she make it past the guards? The queen would never be able to take back the palace because security is incredible tonight. They are former Special Ops! Her own government approved our habitation of the palace, the queen lost and she'll be off

[188]

tending her metaphorical wounds somewhere. *Vassar is just trying to psych me out.* I will not let that happen on my last night in England.

I get the notification that my guest for tonight, famous supermodel Alessandra di Vendeti, is here. She is an Italian heiress who wanted to Partner with the Duke of Cambridge, but he eventually ended up boring her, so she left him. That almost never happens to any Partnership, much less a Royal Partnership.

She is now completely single, and Molly's notification is exactly what I wanted to see.

I go to meet her. She is wearing a blue Valentina dress with subtle frills at the bottom. She's probably 5'11" without heels which means we are about eye-level. My curse is going to be broken. *Marist is missing out.* Why did I just think that? Marist basically left me so her grandmother could Execute me. I kiss Alessandra's hand as I lead her up the grand staircase.

"Will you be giving me the grand tour tonight?" she asks mischievously.

"I wouldn't leave this role to anybody else," I say smoothly.

"What will you be showing me first?"

"The gardens?" I suggest.

She smirks as she grabs the collar of my shirt, moving closer. I know that females all over the globe forget that I cannot feel anything, but I am physically trained to mimic all the emotions associated with sexual

Encounters. My voice drops to a husky whisper. "Perhaps someplace more comfortable?"

"I would like that," she whispers back.

"Here is the broom closet where we here at Buckingham Palace keep the cleaning supplies," I say once we ascend the stairs.

"Is that so?" she laughs.

"Oh yes," I say. "And here is the oldest tapestry in England."

"Really?" she says.

"No, I just made that up. And here, oh…I do not know if I should show you what is behind this door."

Her attention perks up and I smile.

"What is behind this door?" she says as her voice drops.

"This is the Royal Bedroom. This is where the queen would sleep if I had not kicked her out of her palace," I say and she blushes, her skin deepening into a dark red.

"I think I would like to see this room." She brings her eyes back up to look in mine.

"Your wish is my command," I say as I push open the doors.

My SQUAD decorated the entire room and I know one or two cameramen must be in here somewhere; I am used to this. I hold her hand, leading her into the room as we walk over rose petals scattered over the floor. There is light music playing from the speakers hidden in the room and I smell lavender. I am eager to get this show on the road.

"Do you like it?" I ask.

"It is wonderful; how did you do all this? I have never seen anything more beautiful."

"I am looking at something comparable right now," I say, which is a farce, for if she knows anything about Spikes, she must know that we cannot appreciate beauty.

Instead of doubt, though, I observe pure lust. *This is too easy.* I grab her around the hips and bring her over to the bed, slowly lowering her into the sheets, pressing my body against hers. There is no better feeling than pinning my quarry, inhaling someone else's life as you're pressed against one another. She trembles as she interlocks her hands around my head. I quickly check my EYE to make sure this is a good shot because even now, I do not want to diminish the Image. She starts to unbutton my top and presses her hands against my flexed stomach. I grab her bottom lip between my teeth and give a slight pull as her back arches. I reach around to un-zipper the dress from behind but then my night ends with an...

Explosion. The side of the room explodes as an RPG collides with the outside wall of the bedroom. Pieces of the ceiling fall down on our Encounter and I do not have to check to see that the shot is ruined, and my night is over. My ratings are going to fall again. *Dammit.* Redirecting my attention towards the wall, I see it crumble and outside, floating on a hovercraft, is the queen and a dozen of her personal bodyguards. The Duchess makes eye contact with her and rezips her dress as she runs out of the room. *I have completely had it with this woman.*

Her guards jump off the hovercraft and my stomach clenches as something other than adrenaline, surges inside me. My vision turns a deep red and I do not adequately remember what happens next. My vision is so distorted that I use my EYE to see what is going on from outside of me. Almost like I am back in that dream, I see myself spin out of control inside her dressing room. The guards have stepped off the hovercraft but one by one, I dismember them with a sword hanging above the bed. The first two converge on me and it takes no effort to spear and then discard them, as the next two jump towards me.

Grabbing them by the head, I throw them through the gap between the crumbling floor and the hovercraft. I can only assume they fall and break their bodies. *This woman has ruined my entire trip.* My vision continues to get darker. Two more guards charge me and with one clean swipe of the sword, their heads fall off their bodies. The final two guards hesitate before they jump into the room and their hesitation urges me forward. Instead of having them come to me, I jump on the hovercraft and jab the sword up through their chins into their brain, one by one.

It's me and the queen.

"Colman, you don't want to do this!" she screams as I converge on her.

"You went against your word to my handler and tried to Execute me."

"That was a … minor … lapse in judgment on my part. I am sorry!" she yells above the hovercraft engines as tears stream down her face.

"A minor lapse in judgment? A minor lapse in judgment! Are you kidding me?"

She looks behind me and her face regains a semblance of hope. Molly is standing there.

"Colman, you cannot do this," Molly shouts. "This is entirely against Country regulation. What she did was awful, but you cannot retaliate. You must act rationally."

At the last word my entire Being relaxes and I start to see normally again. *Rationally.* Whatever just passed over me disrupted the normal flow of blood to my major organs, it had to. I slightly relax and think about that word. *Rational.* Rationality is how I was made. It is how I act. It is what guides my decisions. Rational thinking is a science. Emotion is a heuristic decision which means it only provides shortcuts to decisions. I am happy that I do not have those to deal with. All my decisions would take so much longer if that was the case. I begin to lower my sword when the queen reaches into her dress and pull out what looks like a gun.

[Weapon Detected. Options Calculating. Calculated. Options: 1. Disarm, 2. Execute, 3. Terminate Existence. Recommendation. Option 2.]

I am not going to be Executed today.

I raise my sword and bring it arching up and over the queen. A look of absolute fear crosses over her face and then...peace. *Peace?* Yes, it is what that looks like. The blade of my sword splits her skull and ruptures her brain. It enters her neck cavity next, passes through the spine, and I hear a scream from somewhere behind me. Molly drops on the floor, screaming and crying at the same time. The blade continues its arc past the queen's neck and breaks her rib cage as it sections her torso in two. Getting past her ribs, the sword finally makes its way through her lower region and the body splits evenly down the middle, falling to either side.

She is Executed immediately and both sides of the former queen roll off the hovercraft. [Encounter. Target Neutralized.] In slow motion, I drop the sword and take one step back onto the bedroom floor. Without the queen controlling the hovercraft, it spirals out of control and careens toward the courtyard. I look back at Molly who is on the floor screaming. I just killed the Queen of England. It was not an emotional decision.

It was rational.

CHAPTER 19

The hovercraft spirals out of control and crashes on the palace steps, spewing fire everywhere. My hands are trembling like leaves in the wind, conceptualizing the decision I just made. What happened to me? Something else – something unexplainable – happened during my decision-making process. That was the first decision of its kind. *What does that even mean?* I have never experienced a psychological response from an Execution before.

I killed a queen as she pulled a gun on me. I was not trained to pick any option other than the rational option. *She pulled a gun and I defended myself.* Molly is moving in slow motion as she runs from the room. Is she leaving me? None of my senses are working properly.

The fire starts licking the steps of the palace and the Special Ops are running around, screaming into their Phase 2 EYEs requesting for backup and evacuation. Bringing their concealed weapons out of their jackets, in the hopes of disabling the villain who tried to enter the palace, they start shooting at the wreckage in a flurry of chaos. I take one step backward, trying to remove myself from being hit with the electric bullets, but they find me before I process what I am doing.

As I fall backwards, two hands cup my armpits and pull me back from the crumbling floor of the former queen's room. The electricity from the weapons have caught the curtains on fire and the room begins to fill with smoke. Trying to turn around, to see whoever is holding me, I discover that moving my head is impossible. *Am I paralyzed?* A shadow falls over me; I cannot make out who it is because the fire is too bright. The only thing I recognize is long brown hair cascading over her face. She drops me and leaves me on the floor. I can't move and my mouth is not opening for me to call for help.

The fire is creeping closer to me and I will myself to initiate the artificial pathways for my legs, but my EYE is offline. *I need help.* I have never thought that before. *I need help or I am going to burn alive.* The wind is howling through the open hole in the side of the room, pushing the fire back from me. The guards are still firing into the room from the ground and the floor is steadily disappearing around me like crumbs falling off a cake. I manage to scream when my brain finally starts working. Immediately the sound of boots on granite echo somewhere from outside the room as my death crawls toward me. Turning my head, what seems like an eternity later, Downey, Fanto, Cassidy, then Rosen appear in the doorway and bolt towards me. *They have to protect me.* Where did Molly go? Cassidy pulls me back as the floor crumbles where I was just lying, and something is injected into my neck. I can move but I still cannot hear.

My EYE turns on and messages start flooding in from Keepers and Producers around the globe. My ratings have reached an all-time high: 13 points from one Encounter. I stand back up as my security forms a box around me and ushers me out of the room. The cameramen and women hiding in the room have abandoned their hiding spots and are trying to film what is going on while simultaneously fighting for their lives as ancient history bursts into flames. Cassidy is in my face screaming at me and mouthing something that looks like: 'We have to move.' *It is time to move.* We sprint out of the bedroom and are greeted by complete pandemonium as the other occupants of the palace flee for their lives.

Molly is screaming at the bottom of the stairs, pushing people out of her way. Where is she going? *I am right here.* What else is she looking for? Executing the queen was a rational decision. Her death should have reduced the loss of life. It should not be causing a panic. Surely my EYE computed the expected outcomes. Did it not expect the hovercraft to spin out of control? *I made a rational decision.* I must have. Finally arriving to the bottom of the stairs, Molly appears from a closet carrying a small wooden box and waves my team forward.

I must not be moving fast enough because Downey and Rosen hoist me onto their shoulders like a baby. The entire palace is empty as the fire snakes down the stairs. Survival instinct kicking in, I squirm my way out of my security's grasp and burst forth from the front entrance. *I Executed the queen.* I am burning one of the most iconic palaces left on the planet. I made the rational decision. That is not supposed to happen. *Surely my EYE calculated all the expected outcomes.*

The hovercraft is still burning when I appear from the crumbling palace and the flames are curling towards the sky. Cars are zooming out the gates with no regard for royal protocol. I see a gaping hole in the side of the palace where the queen's bedroom used to be. There is nothing left of it. The entire façade crumbles and I throw up on the steps. *I made a rational decision.* This should not have turned out this way. Three cars appear out of nowhere. One of my SQUAD gets too close and presses his camera into my face. I take it out of his hand and throw it to the ground. He says something but I still cannot hear. My team ushers me into the car. I am thrown in and no sooner do I hit the seat, than the car takes off. What happened to Molly? Where did all the Sivs go?

I sit in the car alone with no one to tell me what is going on. I am staring at the driver through his mirror and he looks at me. He rolls up the divider. I am sitting in silence, staring out the window as the buildings fall away and are replaced with the English countryside. This is where I saw Marist for the first time. *I made a rational decision.* The palace was not supposed to burn down, my EYE would have taken that into account. *Why did it glitch?* The Special Ops must have misfired and caused the hovercraft to explode. The hovercraft was not meant to crash. How was I supposed to know it would spiral out of control? *My EYE should have told me*. That should have been an expected outcome.

My EYE continues to light up with notifications. I turn it off. I am completely alone. I see the tarmac. How did we make it to the airport? I put my EYE back on and check the time. It is 1 AM. How long have I been in the car? What happened? Where did my team go? Who is opening the door? I am ripped out of the car. I look around, still confused. I see my jet in front of me. My SQUAD is not waiting for me to board and they shovel their gear into the cargo hold. Molly is holding my hand, dragging me towards my cabin. What happened to the palace? Did the queen's body burn? Where are we going?

Just days ago, I Executed a pilot on these jet steps. I bashed her head against the side of the jet until it split open. Molly is still talking to someone on her EYE. She has dropped the bag she is carrying and is shoving me towards the steps. I take the first step. The second step. The third step. Then I look back. In the distance I see red, blue and white lights flashing. Is this the British Military? It is their fault this is happening. *I made a rational decision*. I should have received all possible outcomes to the Execution.

Molly's eye widens as the lights attract her attention. She yells something to my SQUAD, my security team, and the Press. They start loading their equipment double time. I walk into the main cabin. Where are the pilots? Molly starts shaking me. Her mouth is still moving. I cannot hear what she is saying. My name forms on her lips and I snap back into reality.

"Colman!" she screams maniacally. I hear her words. They hit me like a ton of bricks as my dulled senses spring back to me. I am hit with smells, sounds, tastes, and physical sensations all at once. Blood is dripping down the back of my throat. I feel the salt on my tongue. How long have I been like this?

"Colman!" Molly screams again. This time I respond.

"Yes, Molly?" I say dully.

"What have you been doing? Your systems have been down for an entire two hours. I thought I was going to have to resort to a manual EYE restart!"

"What's happening?"

"What do you mean what's happening? You killed the Queen of England and burned down her palace! We have to leave before we are detained here for terrorism charges!"

"I did the rational thing."

"What? How can you say you did the rational thing?"

"She pulled a gun on me."

"She pulled her purse out of her robes!"

"She pulled a gun on me. It was not a purse."

"She pulled a purse! A purse! A *purse*!"

Molly scrambles for her Communication tablet as the two pilots, who look completely sleep deprived and a little drunk, clamber into the cockpit.

"Are we all good to go?" Molly asks now a little more calmly.

"Yes, ma'am," one of them slurs. They are drunk. This is going to be so much fun.

"Then get this bird in the air. We have three minutes before the tarmac gates are breached."

The engines whir to life and I look out the window thinking how different our departure is from our arrival. I almost start laughing. My SQUAD is screaming at each other and my security throws their equipment in the cargo hold. One by one, I see all of them sprint up the steps and Fanto closes the cargo door. The plane starts moving but she is still on the pavement. I tell Molly that Fanto is not inside yet, but she ignores me. She is willing to leave a member of the team on the ground. I watch helplessly as the plane starts moving towards the first runway and Fanto sprints alongside. Out the back entrance, the other three have formed a human chain attempting to reach her. *Please, grab her and bring her in.*

"I am going to break this window and throw myself out of it if this plane does not slow down right now," I yell.

"We do not have time! What is wrong with you?" Molly shouts back.

"I am serious. You two up front, the drunk ones, slow this plane down right now. We have a woman on the ground and the other cabin door is not closed!" I scream.

"Yes, sir."

"No! Do not do that!" Molly screeches.

The military has just entered the parking lot of the private terminal and are wheeling towards the tarmac gate.

"Ma'am, Mr. Cai makes the final decision."

I look back outside and Fanto is scrambling towards the jet's open door. Rosen emerges and extends his hand towards Fanto as she runs.

"Sir, we have to move soon. We will not have time for a safe takeoff," the co-pilot says.

"Ten more seconds," I say.

"Yes, sir."

Fanto has caught up with the plane and is reaching towards Rosen who fumbles with her hand. *Grab it!* This time she grabs it and is hoisted up and over the first two steps. The cars have now reached the tarmac.

"Time to move. Move! Move! Move!" I yell.

The cabin door is not yet shut but I know someone will be working on that as we taxi towards the runway. Sure enough, four sets of hands reach out to hoist the stairs as bullets ricochet off the plane's exterior. The cars are less than 300 feet away and a few Queen's Guard balance themselves out the windows holding semi-automatic guns.

"Yes!" I scream as Molly slaps me in the face. I don't care; I love this adrenaline. Once the steps are completely inside the plane, the jet resumes its path towards the empty runway. Bullets continue to bounce off my window and I feel so happy; how quickly this night turned around! First, I was physically numb and basically unconscious and now I am in a gunfight taxiing in a jet. The G-Force of the takeoff pushes me back into the seat as the jet picks up speed. One of the cars gets too close to the engine and erupts in flames. It explodes with all its sunshine and glory as we lift off the runway. What a night. What a day. *I made a rational decision.* The queen pulled a gun on me. *I made a rational decision.*

"Now what?" I ask Molly.

"Shut up, Colman. I am still trying to figure that out."

"Have you spoken to anybody?"

"Have you spoken to anybody?" she whines, mimicking me. "Colman shut up. You almost cost your entire production crew their lives and all you can say is, 'Now what?'"

"I did not mean that at all. You know it. Should I remind you who the boss is here?"

"I am!" she screams hysterically as she slaps me in the face again. The pilots shut their door. "I am the boss here, you little prick. Shut your mouth. I have saved your life over and over again and all you can do is threaten me with your little power-move of reminding me who the boss is! How dare you? With all that I am doing for..."

"You are so disrespectful, change your attitude!" I bark and this makes her even shriller.

"Excuse me? I have given my life for you, you ungrateful, insolent little brat. I have sacrificed a family, I have sacrificed love, I have sacrificed children, I have sacrificed a normal life... to care for you!"

"What?" I say, alarmed. She just said she 'cared' for me. Adore me, worship me, fine, but don't 'care' for me. No one 'cares' for me.

"I have done everything in my power to make sure that you have all the best clothes, the best food, the best security team, the best Press, the best security detail, the best cars, the best apartment ... and all you can do is say, do this for me, do that for me, make this happen, make that happen. 'Oh Molly, I want to go to England this weekend', 'Oh Molly I want to go to this party', 'Oh Molly can I get that car', 'Oh Molly...', 'Oh Molly...'. It's not all about you, Colman. You may think it is, the world may think it is ... but it's not. You were bred into this life. I had to work for this! We all had the opportunity to have normal lives, but we chose to give that up for you!"

I am so confused. I thought this life is exactly what she wanted. She made a rational decision to be my handler and manage every role in my life. Doesn't that make her happy? She has always just ... been there. I have never thought about her life outside of mine and I do not know what to say back to her.

"Close your eyes and I will alert you when I know what the next move will be. I did not have a contingency plan if you happened to kill the queen and burn down the palace."

"Caring is against regulation," I mutter.

"What?" she says, snapping out of her daze. She went from furious to fearful in no less than one second.

"You said you have sacrificed everything in your life to care for me. That is against regulation."

"I did not say that," she mumbles, fiddling with her Communication tablet.

"I can play it back on my…"

"Enough! I asked you to go to sleep. I do not care about you! I said I 'take care of' you. Didn't I? well I meant that anyway." *She didn't and she knows it.* "That is within regulation. In fact, it's my job. I couldn't give a crap what happens to you. You are replaceable! If you die, then I find someone new! Do you understand that? People all over this Spike-forsaken world want me to work for them because I'm the best damn handler in this world. But I have stayed with this team, time and time again, because I have worked hard to get you where you are."

"Fine," I say, slumping back in my seat.

Her face softens and for the first time, she looks so much older.

"Please, go to sleep. I will wake you when we land," she says softly.

I close my eyes and drift to sleep. This is the first time in a very long time that I will not have slept in my Tube.

I made a rational decision tonight.

Is Marist ok? The queen had it coming. She pulled a gun on me. Alessandra will always remember this night. I wonder how the broadcast turned out if none of my SQUAD was actively managing and editing the shots. Vassar was telling the truth. Molly said she cared about me. It was probably a slip of the tongue. She asked me to kill Marist. Why? I have never been in a gunfight before. They are banned in the Country. I wonder what punishment I will get from Khan. He must not be happy about this Execution. This couch is soft. I wonder how much money was spent on this jet for me. It was custom made. Did the bullets make dents? I wonder if Marist is speeding along the countryside right now...

CHAPTER 20

"Colman, wake up," Molly says.

It is a totally different experience waking up like this and not suffocating.

"I am up," I say as I lift myself off the couch.

"We are back at Obama International and we will have a Press briefing once we get back to the apartment. You have to apologize to the English government. After we go to the apartment, we have to wait for instructions to see where Khan wants to meet us. He called me right after we took off. He is not happy."

"I got it, thank you," I say, thinking back to what Molly said last night. "Molly, thank you for doing this for me. I know how tired you probably are, and this makes my life so much easier. I appreciate you."

"I appreciate the effort. We do not have to talk about it now."

"Colman! Colman! Colman! Colman!"

The national Press is yelling at me as I walk from the plane to the car. "You look like crap! What happened last night? Why did you decide to Execute the queen? What happened to Buckingham Palace? Are you involved with Alessandra? You look awful! Do you know what happened to your ratings last night? Your Profile is holding the number 1 spot! Is this a new fashion style you are wearing? Will you be going back to England any time soon?"

I spend the entire ride in silence. At least it's good to be home. The only thing that makes me feel better is the New York City skyline. The skyscrapers are man-made wonders and 220 Central Park South glimmers in the distance. Bella and Roberto are there.

We arrive right on time; the Sivs in front of my building go crazy when they see the cars pull up. Even at 100% blood capacity, I am tired and not in the mood, but I mount my award-winning smile as I exit the car. The building security cannot keep them back as I exit the vehicle and soon, I am surrounded by screaming male and female Sivs. Fanto, Downey, Cassidy and Rosen do their best to clear a path but after the events that transpired in the past twelve hours, they have no chance. I pose for pictures, sign autographs, and do the usual routine. When I am within thirty feet of the door, my sleeve is gently but insistently tugged on. Standing next to me is the kid with the bright blues eyes and he is all alone.

"Aren't you the little boy from the racetrack in England?" I ask.

"Yes."

"How did you get to New York?"

"I flew."

"Is your family here?"

"No, you Executed them."

Right. I forgot.

"How did you get here?"

"I flew, I was on a jet."

"Did you fly alone?"

"No."

"Whose jet did you take?"

"I was on your jet."

I pause. "What?"

"I flew on your jet to get here."

"Are you here with anyone?" I say sheepishly because this is a really bad prank.

"No, you Executed everyone I loved."

Tough luck. They should not have paid to come after me.

"I do not have time for this. I'm sorry. I have to go into my apartment now."

Security is stationed in the lobby while Molly prepares the Press. I get behind the podium and ask for the first question.

"Colman, there have been rumors…"

"Let me cut you off right there," I sigh. "Rumors are rumors. If you have a specific question, please ask next time. Next!" I shout.

"Colman, was this a premeditated act? Were you going to Execute her all along? The professionals in charge of the crime scene say that the queen was not carrying any type of weapon on her. No gun was found anywhere in the wreckage, yet you Executed her on the premise of self-defense. Can you explain?"

It was a rational decision. I had no other choice.

"This was not a premeditated Execution. She threatened me; I saw the handle of a gun. As you all know, my EYE cannot analyze strike options in the time it takes to fire a bullet – so whether you think it's fair or not, they are not allowed in Encounters against me. That's the law. I abide by all regulations, why should anyone else be different? I have been trained to recognize all forms of weapons and what I saw was the hilt of a gun. This was an unplanned but rational Execution."

"Do you feel any remorse to your decision?"

How absurd. Asking a Spike if he feels remorse? "If I understand your question correctly and understand the definition of remorse – which is 'deep regret or guilt for a wrongfully committed act' – my answer is exactly what I just said before. This was not a wrongfully committed act as this was an act of self-defense…"

"But she did not pull a gun."

"That fact does not matter, what registered on my EYE was a gun," I say.

"How were you not able to tell what she was pulling? The Execution report says the only thing on her person was some type of file. We find it very unlikely that your technology would mistake a file for a gun. I feel like that is a very easy distinction to make."

"That is enough. You are spinning this conversation in circles, to make it seem like this was a premeditated event. That is not what happened. Next question."

"Colman, what is it like have your own handler betray you and let the queen try to Execute you?"

I look at Molly. She did not betray me. To betray is to expose a person to danger by giving the enemy the information they need to do so. Molly said she had no clue the queen was going to do this. *She would not lie to me about this.*

"Molly did not betray me. The queen went against her word and lied to my staff to put me in a position of danger. If you saw the highlight tapes, I did exceedingly well in that Encounter anyway, so it did not make a huge effect on me."

"Sir, we have tapes of palace conversations which the English government just released. We have Molly, on record, agreeing to bring you to the racetrack to ride out on a horse alone ... before a single other Being was allowed out."

Molly looks like a statue. I wouldn't be able to read an emotion on her face if I tried. The queen went back on her word that she wouldn't try anything. Molly couldn't have known that she would do that.

"I stand by my original point. Molly did not know this was coming..."

"We also obtained a recording from a conversation after your last dinner in the palace. We have not gotten rights to it or I would share it with you now."

What? Molly still isn't moving but her face is getting red. Why isn't she doing anything? Accusations like this would normally ruin a handler's reputation. *She must think I am able to handle this all by myself.*

"You are insinuating that Molly led me to my Execution at the racetrack."

He smiles and looks directly at Molly, who stares right back at him. "Yes, that is exactly what I am saying. The evidence shows as much."

"If you can give me the tapes as proof then I will reconsider my answer but right now the logical decision is to answer on the information that I am aware of. Thank you. Next?"

"What happened at the palace is now a global disaster. Alpha Spikes will probably be banned in Britain indefinitely. How is it that you caused such a mess on your trip? Burning down one of the oldest remaining structures on the globe is not something that the world is taking lightly."

"My conclusion and the sensitivity analyses proceeding the event shows that I am not liable for the burning of the palace and neither is the Country. It indeed is a very unfortunate event that we lost Buckingham Palace, but the fault is entirely on England. Next…"

"How did the queen get past the Special Ops in the first place? Part of your camera crew was right outside the place just minutes before she arrived. So were the Special Ops. Records indicate they all deserted the exact area two minutes and thirteen seconds before she arrived."

"That cannot be right," I say shaking my head. They just want a rise out of me.

"Yes, it is. We are trying to obtain the Communication logs between the camera crews, the Special Ops, and the higher level of clearance in your team but the government is rejecting the appeal."

"You are probably mistaken. I am certain that this was just a minor lapse of judgment."

"You're wrong."

"Excuse me?" I say, surprised. No one talks back to me.

"Colman, we have the video logs of all the Special Ops receiving a message two minutes and thirteen seconds before the queen arrived to evacuate the spot right when the queen broke into the palace. The only thing that is missing is why your own team evacuated that area. That seems like an unlikely coincidence."

There is nothing to say to that. I briefly wondered why the queen was able to breach security. Only Molly or one of my personal security would have had the clearance to give that order.

"That's enough. I have nothing to say to that accusation. I am sure you will receive the truth eventually."

"But..."

"Enough! Next person, fire away."

"Sir, we have seen your ratings tank and then skyrocket. Do you believe that this trip was just a ploy to attract more attention to your Image?"

"That is the only thing this trip was about. What else would a visit to England be about?"

"There are rumors … sorry, there is a common belief circulating that this trip was created for the sole purpose of seeing the princess."

"I do not know anybody stupid enough to believe that. Who here believes that?" I say jokingly.

Almost everyone raises their hands.

"Wow, ok then. Well, you should be doing your research."

"Sir, it seemed like you and the princess Marist shared a very special moment in the bathroom. Then she did not come out in public when you had an Encounter on the racetrack. What was this about? Are you falling for the princess?"

What an absurd question. To the best of my knowledge the socially denotated phrase 'to fall' means to have feelings for some other Being.

"I am one of the only Alphas on the globe and you are going to ask me if I am 'falling for' a Siv princess?"

"Yes."

"Are you aware that the only types of sensations I experience are physical, not emotional?"

"Yes, but Australian scientists just published research showing that they used Nalgene-521to unlock actual emotional reactions in Spikes and…"

"And we are done here," Molly butts in, snapping out of her trancelike state from before. "Thank you, everyone, for your time. I am here to answer any other questions you may have. Colman has a very important appointment with the Super this evening that he must prepare for."

I make my way off the stage, even though the Press is still screaming crass questions at me, because Molly made it very clear that this discussion is over. They are very conspiratorial today. Molly would not try to Execute me. She said that it was not my day to be Executed the night before the racetrack. I have known her for years now and even if she doesn't care about me, her job is to protect me. And her job is her life. *Right?*

I ride the elevator all the way up to my penthouse and a physical relief sweeps over me as I enter the room. It is good to be back. I call for Bella and Roberto and they come running around the corner of the wall like two little dogs hearing the sound of food hitting their bowl. It is great to see them.

"Colman, Colman, good to see you, baby. It has been so long," Bella says.

"A couple days? It is great to see you, too, Bella. Roberto how are you, my man?"

"Oh Colman, Roberto is so good. So good to see you as well. We watched your Encounter with those evil doggies and the horsemen and Roberto got a little nervous, but I knew you could handle yourself."

"I am so glad that you two have confidence in me. I was disappointed that you only stayed one day in England, nothing was the same without either one of you."

"You are too respectful sir, too respectful."

"We here now and ready to work."

"Then I say we get this show on the road. I have an appointment with the Super tonight to discuss everything that has happened…"

"Oh, we know. We have been given special instructions. Roberto and Ms. Bella have everything already laid out for you, sir. We do not agree with the instructions, but we must follow," Roberto says.

"Then what do we have assigned for tonight?"

"Sir, you have an all-white Hugo Boss suit."

"Really?" I say excitedly.

"Sir, we do not like this."

"Why?"

"We do not want to frighten you."

"Why would you frighten me?"

"We have a bad feeling about tonight, that's all," Bella says quietly.

"I'm sure everything will be fine. The Super will probably just draw a little blood to make it known that he does not condone the actions in England. I am sure it will be fine."

"Oh, yes, sir," Roberto adds quickly, looking at Bella.

"Me no meant to frighten you, sir."

"You wouldn't be able to even if you tried," I say lightheartedly.

They look at me sympathetically, but I barely notice it because Roberto has brought out the suit for the evening. Damn, they really were not kidding. It's so white it's practically glowing. It is completely spotless, and the lapel is a bright silver. Interesting … it almost reminds me of Jack the Ripper.

"Ms. Bella added some secret things to the suit," Roberto says.

"Yeah, yeah but you must not say nothing to nobody. Sneaky, yeah?" Bella adds.

I nod, not knowing what that really means but enjoying what I am looking at.

"Thank you, both of you. I am very happy that I have you two in my life."

Bella tears up and Roberto gives her a gentle rub on her back. It almost reminds me of how they behaved in that dream… but, no, that couldn't be.

"Sir, we must go now. Maybe you need night in tonight, yes? You no go out."

"Roberto agrees, Colman. We think you need to rest. You cannot go to Khan in the Black Mansion tonight. It would not be good for your health."

"Thank you, both of you. But I'll be fine. Enjoy your evening."

My response ends the conversation and they know better than to press me. Just before they leave, they both look at me with a type of pity. I mean, I know that the suit is not my normal style, but it is really not that bad. Plus, I cannot wait to see the special alterations Bella made.

CHAPTER 21

"That was an absolute disaster," Molly exclaims as she and security file out of the elevators.

"Why was everyone pinning all these conspiracies on you?"

"I have no clue, but it is not something we should worry about now … what is that?" Molly says pointedly looking at the suit. "Pretty snazzy."

"Bella and Roberto just left…"

"Yes, I saw them exit. Why was Bella crying?"

"What? She was crying?"

"Yes."

"I don't know. I don't think I said anything. They said they received special instructions from Khan's team to make sure I show up tonight in a white suit."

Molly's face drops and she turns pale.

"Is everything ok?" I say, sensing her apprehension.

"Yeah, no, yeah, I mean, no everything is fine."

"Molly, maybe you should try to reschedule this meeting until you can talk to the Super's team about what actually happened in England?" Downey says from the back.

Molly nods. "Downey, what a great idea. Let me try to make the call right now." With that, she scuttles away.

"Sir, there is something you should know…" Rosen says.

"Hold on, I am sorry I have to take this," I say as my EYE flashes.

I walk into my room where my Tube has been reconfigured and there is a notification saying that it is from the London area.

"Colman!" Marist's voice echoes in my head. Every time she speaks, my stomach does a little flip. I must not have had enough to eat today, and my brain must be associating her voice with a lack of safety. *That is the rational explanation.*

"Marist, where have you been? Thanks for sacrificing me."

"Colman, I do not have much time. I was locked in my room that day. I heard Molly talking to my grandmother after dinner that night and heard them agreeing to Execute you."

"What?"

"Colman – Molly and my grandmother were working together."

"That is impossible," I breathe.

"You need to listen to this tape. Is this line secure?"

"Of course."

"Ok, here goes…"

I hear Molly's voice.

"It is just not rational, Your Majesty. He will not go down without a fight."

"You are quite right, and I am quite aware," the queen responds, "but you should remember who makes the regulations in this country."

"Your Majesty, I meant no disrespect. It's just - allowing you to do anything to him while he is abroad would greatly damage and change the way Sivs around the world view Spikes. It will affect my standing within the Country. I will not sacrifice that just to appease you."

"Watch your tone. I am not someone who would offer up nothing in return for this great sacrifice. I would be willing to offer you a position within my administration for the remainder of your life. You would not be able to return to the Country, but you could start a new life in England after it is over."

"That is a very kind offer, Your Majesty, but I will not be accepting. I have great upward mobility within the Country. I hope to one day design Spikes as a Keeper. It has been a lifelong goal of mine."

"Molly, I am not someone that Beings say no to. There is a very good reason for this. Please take tonight to reconsider your answer and if it changes please tell me in the morning. The Guineas Stakes will take place as planned, regardless of your answer, so if you don't change your mind, that will be the last event we invite you to attend in England."

"Thank you, Your Majesty. We are going to be leaving tomorrow anyway," Molly says.

"Take one moment and consider this option with a little more depth to it," the queen says, almost pleading.

"How do you mean?"

"You must know the current political climate in the Country."

"I am very well aware."

"Then you have heard the rumors about what is happening on the other side of the globe."

"I have."

"What do you think of them?"

"I do not need to think of them."

"He is the only Alpha in the Country."

"I know."

"Then you know why that is."

"Nothing is confirmed."

"Would you rather free him now when there is still hope left or let the Country do it?"

"I cannot answer that question. I do not care about him."

"Do not lie to yourself, dear. I have been alive long enough to know when an administration is going to fall, and I am sure that you care tremendously for this young Spike that you have created from the ashes. Why do you think I removed all the other positions in my government when we were attacked? He is the Country's last hope and they are going to use him in every way imaginable. You have the opportunity to release him."

"By Executing him?"

"If you say so. Please, you have a key to my room tonight. You are required to come up."

"I will not reconsider."

"It is mandated. I will talk to you tonight. Thank you."

Before I even have time to process the conversation, Marist feeds the conversation from later that evening.

"Have you reconsidered my offer?" the queen says.

"Yes, I have," Molly says without hesitation.

"I knew you would. In order for this to work, I must be kept alive. I know that he is going to come after me for doing this and your position in my administration is available as long as I am alive."

"I know, Your Majesty."

"Then we are in agreement?"

"Yes."

"Tomorrow at the racetrack what will your job be?"

"I will send Colman out on the horse of his choosing and then will leave him for your Spikes to capture him…"

"That's a good girl. You will be an excellent Foreign Secretary."

"Thank you," Molly says, and the conversations ends.

What did I just hear? There is a strange weight on my heart. *Molly did try to Execute me.* My own handler was actively trying to Execute me. That is totally irrational. I am her lifeline. I make her money. I make her Famous. I give her a purpose. She shouldn't be trying to Execute me. This does not make any sense. But I just heard it.

"Marist, how did you get that?"

"Colman, I am so sorry. I can't imagine how you must be feeling."

"I do not feel anything."

"I don't know what to tell you."

"How did you get that tape?" I ask again.

"I tapped the queen's bedroom thinking something like this was going to happen. I wanted to keep you safe."

"She is really trying to Execute me." I bet this is when people feel betrayed.

"I'm sorry."

"Who are you?" I blurt out. "Why have you been doing this? Who do you work for?"

"I wish I could answer that now, I really do, but I will be over to help you soon. I promise."

The connection ends.

This is why I am glad I don't feel anything; it would make it harder to pretend. My smile is going to still shine through my eyes when I walk back into that room.

I am going to have to Execute Molly before she Executes me.

She is a direct threat to my existence. Is my security team in on this? The liquid she injected in my Tube before the race was probably something to make me perish more quickly. My hand did not heal the day after Marist burned it! It must have been an anti-hemorrhaging liquid. She tried to make it easier for me to bleed out! I must go back out there to face all of them. I need to figure out the rational thing to do. Separating the real team from the fake team.

"Colman, are you alright in there?" Molly calls from the other room.

"Yes! All set; just had to jump on a call with one of the duchesses from England," I say as I walk back into the other room.

I am smiling from ear to ear, even though I know I must Execute the one person who has gotten to me where I am today.

CHAPTER 22

"How did the call go with Khan's team?" I ask. My smile is plastered on my face. If I could feel anything, I imagine it would hurt.

She looks at Downey. *Is Downey in on this too?*

"I could not reschedule."

"There must be a way to reschedule," Downey interjects.

Downey is trying to ambush me but pretending like she is supporting me.

"Unfortunately, there is nothing I can do. We will all have to proceed as planned," Molly says.

"That's fine. Are all of you going to be coming tonight?"

"Yes," they say in unison.

"Very well then. Let's not waste time. I need someone to help me get into this suit. Khan's palace is a four-hour shuttle and we do not want to be late, do we?"

I am getting annoyed; this is a production and they are not doing anything to get me ready.

"Rosen get my chair. Downey grab my suit. Fanto, I need you to grab the combs and pomade. Cassidy, go get my makeup. Honestly, why did Bella and Roberto leave so early?"

They all scatter, and Molly stands there like she doesn't know what to do. Normally, she's the one giving those orders.

"Molly, can I help you with something?"

"Uh, no. I'm fine. Thank you."

"Then put yourself to good use and grab me something to eat."

"Colman, I don't think you should go tonight."

"You just said yourself - that is not up to you."

"You could personally call his people."

"Come on now, don't get soft on me. Khan will probably draw a little bit of blood and that will be it. I have handled more than my fair share over the past five days, haven't I? Now, I gave you an order. Go get my food," I spit, immediately turning away so she can't see my face.

My tone will be the least of her problems tonight. The rest of my staff gathered what I asked of them and I start getting dressed into my white ensemble. Afterwards, I think this pick is perfect for the occasion. The silver lapel makes my blue eyes look electric.

"Where's the camera crew?" I ask.

"I did not think you wanted them up here after the press conference, so we got approval to make them stay downstairs."

"No, no, come on now. It is time to give the people a show. I'm back in the Country and ready to party!"

"I'll call them up right now," Molly says happily.

Minutes later, my SQUAD is scrambling out of the elevators with their cameras and indoor boom mics, all ready to go. They take their positions around the room.

I am going to send a warning for anybody who has ever thought about double-crossing me.

"I need two cameras on me. One of you get a side shot," I say as I walk over to stand in front of my huge one-story windows. "And one of you get a shot of me from behind. It's time to start the main show."

"Sir, would you like to call the shots for this, or do you want us to move based on what we think?"

"You do whatever you think. However, I am going to adjust the collar of my shirt and when I do that I want you back in your original positions. Got it?"

"Yes, sir. Tell us when you are ready."

"You can air in 3 … 2 … 1."

On one, I turn around and look out the window. The shot on my EYE looks incredible; the sun is just begging to set over NYC and the white tux is reflecting so much light that I look like an angel.

"I wanted to begin tonight's streaming by telling everyone what happened in England and update all of you what I will be doing from here on out," I say as I turn around. "Rumors are floating around that do a great disservice to the surviving royal family and to myself so I will dispel them one by one. The first is that the queen did not have a gun. Let me be clear on this:

[227]

she *absolutely* had a gun. I am releasing a logistics report detailing the entire circumstance. The British authorities tried to pretend that the queen had some sort of file to make me look like the villain but that is a fruitless attempt at undermining me. Do not try to blame an outsider when the actual problem is under your very noses. The queen was a self-obsessed, lustful bitch who, when she could not get something she wanted, tried to take it by any means necessary. I was a guest of honor and they did not treat me as such."

My security guards are practically pooping their pants.

"As for the recent allegations that Princess Marist and I are partners. This will continue no longer. That is an easily refutable claim made up by people who know nothing about my species. The Spike species was created to entertain all of you who are watching now. If you do not respect us, and me, then try and come for me. I will Execute you myself."

A notification from Molly arrives on my EYE. I push it out of the way, and I continue.

"England is highly irresponsible and from this point on I will not be asked about this again. Is this clear?"

I stare hard into the cameras and make sure that even though no one can respond to me, the power displayed on my face is visible.

"Now, I do not want to dwell on this anymore so instead, I want to tell you all something very personal about me – to let you in on my life, if you will. If anyone steps in my way from this day onward…"

Two more notifications pop up. One from Molly and one from … Rosen? I look towards him, but he is no longer in the room.

"…I will Execute you without giving a moment's notice. It is time that we all learn to respect those Beings above us. I am above you all. I do not serve you; you serve me."

Four more notifications arrive: one from a Keeper, one more from Molly, one from Downey, and one from Fanto. I look around but other than the two cameramen in my room, no one is here.

"I will show no mercy to any Siv who dares to Encounter me. I am the last Alpha in the Country. If you think that I will go down without some sort of fight, you are gravely mistaken."

My EYE is continually beeping now as notifications flow in from my publicity teams.

"I am here to tell you all," I reach to touch my collar and the cameramen move back into their original positions and I turn back to face the windows, "that I am not a Spike who will abide by any restraints. Any Being who tries to cross me will be slain and hung for the entire world to see. I wish you all a relaxing evening because if you are one of the selected people, it will be your last."

The cameras shut off leaving the world in darkness.

CHAPTER 23

The cameras evacuate the room as I reapply my makeup before I descend from my penthouse. My warning went relatively well. I do not know where everybody went but that's not important. Scrolling through the archives of my Communication, there are numerous 'job well done' messages from Keepers, my security team just alerted me that they were leaving, and then I see Molly's message repeated, 'You are making a mistake.'

This was a rational move.

Every Being must be reminded who is in charge. If there is a belief that they are in charge that could cause a huge power differential and that would turn into a problem for me. I finish applying the last touches of my makeup when, in the corner of the mirror, I see the reflection of two small feet.

"I told everyone to get out," I say as I turn my head.

The little boy from the racetrack is standing in my room.

"How did you get in here?"

"I came up the elevator."

"I am done with this. Who are you?"

"Colman, do you not recognize who I am?"

"No. You told me that I Executed your family."

He stares at me for a moment, his head cocked to the side. There is a smile on his face like he is mocking me. *Me!*

"I am you."

Oh lord, this kid really has a wild imagination.

"Kid, look, I have places to be. You need to get out of this apartment before I have the big bad security team come to get you."

"Do you want to Execute me?"

"No, why would I want to do that?"

"I want to Execute you."

Now this kid has my attention.

"You know that is not possib…"

The kid jumps from the opposite side of the penthouse and pins me against the wall. The impact cracks my mirror and he is gripping my throat so tightly that I immediately start to suffocate.

"I want you to remember this when you meet Khan tonight," he says.

I try to pick him up and slam him against the mirror, but I look into his eyes and see my eyes. My eyes were designed as a one of a kind pair. I am looking at my own reflection.

"Not everything is always as it seems. You will be needing a friend tonight."

"Whoa there … what is…" I gurgle.

He jumps off and scurries into the other room. He is a quick little kid. When I follow him, I see that my Tube is the only object in the room.

He is me? Really? What nonsense.

Making my way into the elevator, I decide that I will let my security take out this little pest. The cracked mirror interestingly reflects the dimming light; there is a beam touching the four corners of the room.

The ding signals my exit and I am once again flooded with light. I assume that I am glowing because I hear sounds of admiration from the elevator lobby. I am greeted by the Press who have probably been waiting here since I left them earlier. Molly moves into my peripheral. [Track Subject. Molly O'Reilly. Range: 10 feet.] I do the same for the rest of the security team. My brain is going to be overloaded with stimuli but I would rather spend a night overworked than Executed.

I make my way through the Press and look towards the double doors where the little boy is standing. He merely smiles. Pulling Cassidy out of formation, I tell him to take another one of our team to find that child and keep him secured. He spots the target and takes Downey with him. I continue to walk and exit the hotel lobby, pose for a few photos outside with a few Sivs, then board a hovercraft to get to Khan's mansion. My team gets in on all sides of me then Molly starts reading the agenda for today.

"At 7:45 PM we will depart 220 Central Park South. It is now 7:44. Okay, we are early, great. Then at 11:45 PM, we will arrive at the Super's mansion. At

12:00 AM, you will meet with Kendall Khan." She sighs.

Yeah that's right, bitch, I evaded you once and I will do it again. Come at me.

"That is all I have. Does everybody copy? Khan did not tell us when the meeting will be over."

"You'd think he would treat his last Alpha Spike with a little more respect than that," I sneer.

"Let's all just enjoy the ride and if we could turn on some music that would be great," Molly says.

Even if I could feel sympathy for her, I wouldn't. It is one thing to schedule Encounters when you are a handler but another to make sure that my possibility of Execution is imminent. Two of the Beings from my SQUAD jump into the hovercraft as we push off the curb; they probably want to get B-roll of me sipping a drink before we get to Khan's. Once the hovercraft is full of people, we stabilize and I notice that while Fanto and Rosen are with me, Downey and Cassidy are in the other one. Molly is sitting directly opposite of me and my SQUAD is sitting next to her. Six is a bit of a crowd. I wonder if Cassidy and Downey caught the kid.

About an hour and a half into the ride, we encounter slight turbulence and are alerted that the weather has changed so we have to make a quick landing to repair one of the boosters. The 5,000-foot descent is not easy, and we land in the middle of a field somewhere in Dirty Jersey. It is called New Jersey but it's anything but new. Climbing out, my SQUAD starts getting a shot of the pilot repairing the hovercraft, Molly deboards and so do the two remaining members of the team. I wonder where the other craft landed. They were right behind us when I checked last.

[Alert. Incoming Missile.]

Only the subconscious response propels me to alert the other members of the team and I scream it for everyone to hear as we scatter into the surrounding area. The hovercraft explodes and although the blast has made me slightly disoriented, Molly is definitely smiling as she looks at my two security guards. Is she checking their response time? She just tried to Execute me. This is enough. I have had enough.

[Alert. Weapon Detected.]

Two metal spikes are embedded in the ground and Molly is eyeing them the same way I am looking at them. She moves more quickly than me. *She knows I caught her.* Molly reaches down and grabs one while I leap for the second. Running towards her from the distance away, she looks prepared to fight me even though she knows I will obliterate her. As I raise the spike to gain enough momentum, Rosen steps in front of her. My arms shake as I stop the momentum in mid-air. I should at least hear him out before I Execute him too. It looks like my entire security team has turned. How unfortunate.

"Colman, -don't," Rosen says.
"Give me one good reason," I respond, coldly.
"She is trying to protect you."
"No, she is not!"

"Yes, I am!" she screams.

"You are not, you want me Executed!"

"That is not what I am trying to do!" she says, defeated.

[Alert. Hovercraft Approaching.]

Out of the grey sky, the second hovercraft is finally landing but when I zoom in, this hovercraft is not carrying anyone I recognize. Fanto and Rosen are blinking their eyes rapidly which I assume is to alert the others of our whereabouts. The hovercraft lands and men dressed in black, who have the Country logo embedded on the front, come running towards me. They aren't hostile so I drop the spike on the ground. Finally, the Country is here. Molly rushes forward to meet them and they bring her to the ground with one charge from their tasers. She lays there spasming on the ground and I smile. Fanto and Rosen try their hand, and although they get a little further, they too end up in the same position.

"It has been my absolute pleasure to have had the ability to interact with all three of you all these years…" I begin to say.

[Alert. Weapon Detected: Gun.]

Out of the corner of my eye, one of the Country Guards take out a gun and shoots the two members of my SQUAD, as well as the pilot, in their heads. They crumble as red chunks fly into the rich earth. Guns are not allowed. Have I made a mistake? Didn't their emblems say they were from the Country? Why do they have guns? More importantly, why did they use them against the cameramen who have done absolutely nothing to threaten them? I stare at the three former members of my team who are lying there, open-eyed, looking at me.

"Sir, you need to come with us for your own safety," the lead-militant says to me.

"Guns are illegal in the Country. No one, regardless of their clearance level, is allowed to have one," I say, and I do not think he really likes this because he holds his up to my head. "You will not be shooting me today. I am sorry to tell you."

"You want to try me?" he smirks.

Another man comes from the pack and whispers something in this man's ear. He drops his gun.

"Sir, you need to come with us for your own safety," he says again.

"Who are you?"

"We are Keepers."

"With the Country?" I say skeptically.

"Yes."

"And you are here because…?"

"We received word that you were in imminent danger."

"And having a gun held up to my head is a less imminent danger?"

"Sir," a sigh. "You need to come with us for your own safety."

"So you keep saying. Tell me where I am going and why I am going."

"Tell him," says the guy behind Mr. Muscles.

"We have been following your hovercraft from above on your way to the Mansion. We noticed when you went down and we followed you. Then we saw your handler pick up the metal spike and came to assist."

"You don't think I could handle a Siv with a metal spike?"

"It was a precautionary measure."

"Why did you Execute the cameramen?"

"We did not know if they were armed."

"Well, at least someone is worried about my physical well-being. Thank you!" I say joyously.

"We are going to escort you to the Mansion ourselves."

I look down at my fallen team. Molly has tears running down her face and the other two are looking at me, despair flooding their eyes.

"As I was saying, it has been my absolute pleasure to have worked with all three of you these past years. You have taught me invaluable lessons, so I have been told, but when I find out that my own handler is actively trying to prepare my Execution, I cannot let that stand," I say.

And with that, I hop into the hovercraft with the new members of my security team – as my former members are loaded into the back.

CHAPTER 24

It takes us less than an hour to fly the remainder of the way and there is no music playing this time. Finally, things are starting to make sense. *It makes rational sense.* Downey and Cassidy must be the loyal ones and Molly needed them out of the way so she planted the kid so I would see him as I exited the lobby, knowing I would dispatch Downey and Cassidy to take care of it.

Molly probably had the second hovercraft destroyed along the way. The new regulation about no radio waves was convenient because I would not have been alerted that the second hovercraft was going down. Molly paid the pilot to land on an unsubstantiated claim over an engine malfunction then would have Executed me while Fanto and Rosen watched me die. It was an ingenious plan, except for the fact that I am a Spike and would have Executed all three of them before they could make any moves on me.

If she did happen to Execute me, she would tell everyone that I fell out of the hovercraft or something - I can only imagine how that headline would go down. She would evoke a considerable vat of sympathy and would be hired as a handler for some other Spike or maybe even be promoted to a Keeper. That would have been beneficial for her. My security team would retire with millions in an offshore account somewhere and this whole mess would not be remembered in five or ten years from now. The headlines would be, 'Freak Accident Takes Life of Violent and Respected Alpha Spike'.

How ironic, that the very people who wanted to Execute me are now going to be Executed. What a life I live.

"Gentlemen, we are starting our final descent. We will be on the Mansion lawn in T-minus four minutes," the pilot says through my headset.

"What time is it?" I ask.

"11:40 PM."

Even though they are of no use to me, when I Execute Molly, I will make sure I tell her that I appreciate how she always kept me on time. This small detail helped me do a lot more in my day than most other Beings could do in theirs. Fanto and Rosen will be thanked for their years of faithful service and I will shake each one of their hands before I behead them. I will save Molly for last so she can see that this is her fault. She should have never made that deal with the queen.

The craft lands precisely three minutes later and my new SQUAD jumps out in a very sharp formation. I like how these guys move. I am pulled from the craft and am half-dragged, half-carried, towards the steps.

"Hold on, hold on there. I am very able and willing to walk. Thank you very much."

"We are following orders."

"If you are going to be my new team then you take orders from me."

"Who said we are going to be your new team?"

"What?" I say but no one responds.

The brilliant Black Mansion looms in front of me. Before 2025, there was a completely white building here, called The White House. Khan said that white was too pure and innocent. He wanted to paint the house in the blood of the people who he Executed from the chemical attacks but one of the Keepers said that the chemicals stored in the blood still could permeate the walls of the house. Light seems to bend toward this house as a black hole would; it is daunting, huge, and very historic. All the perfect things to instill a sense of fear in the people one must Regulate.

[Alert. Unusual Heat Signature Registered.]

I am almost to the front steps when a blur passes in the top right corner of my field of vision, but the doors open before I can get a better look. Standing there in his full glory, smiling through his genetically altered white teeth, is Kendall Khan.

"Ah! The man of the hour. Welcome to my house," he says as he holds his arms out to the side.

"Khan, it is great to see you. Thank you so much for calling the meeting. I thought you were going to be angry about England, but I am glad you are not."

"I am fuming on the inside, but we must not talk about that now. I heard we have three more guests joining us tonight?"

"Yes. I discovered that my handler ... you remember Molly?"

"Yes, yes, how could I forget?"

"Yes well, she and the former Queen of England tried to Execute me," I say coldly. "I can't believe it. I kind of liked her."

He chuckles. "As if you could like anyone."

I nod, conceding. If I could've liked anyone, though, it would've been her. "True."

"What a shame, even so. I would never would have suspected that. The things some people do for Money, Power and Fame am I right?"

I see his eyes watch Molly, Rosen and Fanto being unpacked from the back of the craft. I look after them, something tickling the back of my head. Not regret, necessarily, but *something*. It sucks that they betrayed me. "Certainly."

"We mustn't stand out here. There is much I want to discuss with you tonight and even more I want to show you."

"Very well, lead the way," I say, manufacturing a smile.

"I am certainly glad you were not Executed before you got here, Colman."

"Me too, it has been a hectic day with a lot of twists and turns but I was determined to make it, even though I was asked to cancel this meeting."

[241]

"Why were you asked to cancel tonight?" he asks nervously.

"It is nothing too serious. Molly and one of my security asked me to. They probably wanted to Execute me in my own dwelling," I say, laughing.

"Are you hungry?" Khan says suddenly.

"Very much, what's for dinner?"

"I had only the best prepared for you. Your personal favorites. We have duck, lamb, bone marrow, and bottles of 2004 Domaine de la Romnee Conti. We have a lot to talk about tonight and there is no other way to talk than over a nicely cooked meal."

"I couldn't agree with you more," I say excitedly.

"I must also mention that I was right when I said you would look handsome in an all-white suit," he says as he sizes me up and looks more closely.

"Very well. I am sure you need to do a little clean up before we have dinner brought out. Take twenty minutes for some pre-dinner relaxation and preparation. I will send in one of my stylists right away. We want to make sure you are looking camera ready for a Black Mansion feast now, don't we?" He winks.

"Absolutely, where should I get prepared?"

"I prepared the room at the very end of the hall for you. You just go straight down." He points. "Now don't stray; we don't want you being late for dinner."

"Thank you again for your hospitality."

"There is no need to thank me again … you are doing more for me than you know. Now go get ready!" he says as he waves his hand toward the hallway.

I take my steps in stride. The beginning of my evening may not have worked out but now it's undoubtedly shaping up nicely. Truthfully, I'm a little suspicious but my position as the only Alpha Spike left is my insurance.

I enter my room and the clock reads 12:01 AM. I take a seat in the chair that is in front of the mirror and pick up one of the nature magazines resting on the desk when a door opens.

"I just need a touch-up on my makeup, some cologne, and my shoes need buffing. The Country Guard practically dragged me through the grass in white shoes. I can imagine they are shining a little bit on the greener side today," I say when I hear the door open.

"I will not be helping you with that," Marist says.

I jump up. *How did she get in here*? "Marist, I…"

"You look calm for someone who is about to be Executed," she says.

"So, you are cracking jokes now?"

"Colman, I seriously messed up."

"Hey, aren't I the one who should be apologizing? I killed your grandmother, after all."

"She was going to have you Executed."

"I need explanations, Marist. You need to tell me how you are like … this," I say as I gesture to her.

"We do not have much time. First, Khan brought you here to Execute you. I have no idea why or how but that is what you are doing here tonight."

"That can't possibly be true. The Country makes too much money off me to want me dead."

"I know it makes no sense, but you have to believe me."

"You know, Marist, I'm not a fan of how you keep showing up telling me that I am in danger. In case you have not seen all the footage, I do a pretty good job of staying alive."

"I helped you last time, didn't I?"

"With what?"

"I told you Molly was trying to Execute you."

"Valid point. I will give you that, but this time you are wrong. The worst Khan is going to do is make an overly dramatic performance over whatever he asks me to do."

"Listen to me…"

"No, you listen to me. This conversation is over. A Country stylist will be coming in here any minute and I will not defend you if they see you. I do not know how you made it past the guards to begin with, but it is time for you to leave."

"If you do not want to believe me then you have to take this final bit of information. I am telling you this not because I think you care but because I want to give you the same respect that I would want."

"I hear the stylists coming, you better hurry up."

"Khan has your Donors."

What did she just say? My Donors are dead.

"That is impossible. Marist get out. I have had enough of these lies. Spikes are not allowed to have a family in Country."

The door opens and Marist looks at me as a single tear rolls down her cheek. She bolts through an open window, through which she must have entered. What an absurd thing to say. Khan does not have my Donors. They were Executed before I was even created. These English girls, every one of them is crazy.

"Ah hello, handsome. Colman, it is my absolute pleasure to meet you. I am a huge fan. When Mr. Khan assigned me to work on you, I could not believe my luck. My name is May," a beautiful foreign woman says, extending her hand.

"May ... what a nice name. I am glad they picked you. You are very attractive," I say as she blushes. "May, I just want you to do whatever you think will make me presentable tonight for dinner."

"Of course, sir. I see your shoes are a little dirty. I can have those shined immediately. Let me take those from you." She bends down slowly and picks up my shoes for me.

"Thank you, May. You look like you could use a break. How about if we take these twenty minutes while we wait for the shoes to spend some alone time with each other?"

"It would be my honor. What would you like to start with?" she says slyly.

"Let me slip out of this suit and then we can decide."

"I was hoping you were going to say that," she smiles.

As I go to drape my jacket over the back of the makeup chair, a small rustle peaks my attention from outside the window. Is she back? I feel myself look expectantly but it was just slight breeze. Suddenly, a wave of dizziness washes over me and I feel weird about taking the rest of my clothes off.

"Actually, we should probably get right to work. Kendall is not a very patient man and I do not want to be late for dinner."

"Oh, did I do something wrong?"

"No, I just think a better use of our time spent together would to actually be preparing for dinner, so we do not disrespect his hospitality."

May frowns but she agrees. She begins to retouch my makeup and my shoes are returned basically glowing.

"May, thank you so much for your expertise. It was great meeting you, but my time is almost up and I have to do a few last-minute preparations on my own."

She takes the hint and leaves. Laying down on the bed, my EYE ticks down to two minutes remaining and I think about the people in my life. Molly, Kendall, Cassidy, Downey, Marist, Vassar, Queeny-baby, Rosen, the little boy, and Fanto. How different this life would be if none of them were in it. Then I think about my Donors. I've always wanted to know who, exactly, they were. But they've been dead for a long time.

Haven't they?

Donning my jacket, I make my way back into the hallway and see Khan rounding the corner just in time to greet me.

"Punctual as ever."

"I learned from the best."

"You must have. Now, shall we eat?" Kendall holds out a hand, leading the way.

CHAPTER 25

"The food looks impeccable; my compliments to the chef."

Khan has the only EYE faster than mine. He sends a message on it and two seconds later says, "He says thank you."

"Kendall, what did you want to talk about tonight? What is this about?"

"Funny you should ask. I was just going to ask you the same thing."

I laugh hesitantly. "But I didn't call this meeting." Honestly, after all the weird stuff that has been happening recently, I may be going crazy.

"In a way, you did, Colman. See, I have been watching you for a very long time. In fact, I would go so far as to say that you have been my crown jewel."

"Thank you, sir…"

"Please, Colman, I am not finished," he says sternly. "You are a crown jewel on my long list of accomplishments. I successfully took over half of an entire continent in the midst of chaos, I engineered a new species of Beings, I rule with absolute authority, I have information streaming in from every single State on this miserable globe but you, Colman Cai, were the missing piece."

I stare at him. He might have drunk too much wine. I glance at the various cameramen positioned around the room and notice for the first time that they are wearing body armor. I know Khan is scary but it's not like he's going to Execute a cameraman for no reason.

"You are incredibly powerful, whether you realize it or not. In fact, some would say, more powerful than I. You have people that are willing to die for you, just to touch you – to have seconds alone with you. They are willing to pay for this. You have created Beings who will chop off their hair, tattoo themselves, buy any product you tell them, and create children to ensure that their children will know the incredible stories of Colman Cai. You rule out of fierce respect. When a Siv pays for an Encounter, they know that you will show them a fair fight and end their life with respect. That is something I do not have."

"Why thank you…"

"I am not finished!" he roars.

I sit there, stunned.

"In the face of death, you have found resilience and determination. You make people smile when they see you. You make people faint when they touch you. You cause the Siv mind to do so many things that are otherwise out of their control and you do it unknowingly. This is why you are a crown jewel. You are the perfect weapon."

Say again?

"I brought you here today because I want us to work together to bring the Country into a new Golden Age. We have the firepower and we have the leadership. What we need now is someone to mobilize the masses to wreak havoc on every other State."

Khan is being irrational. Is it just the wine? It wouldn't be a beneficial or strategic move for the Country to weaponize me. We already have a dwindling population; we do not need to lose more people.

"In this time, I will call on you to be the face of the Country. You will be the leader of our military and the face of hope. I know together we will be able to do great things. What do you think of this proposal?

"Are you serio…" I begin.

"Wait, before you answer that - I have brought some special guests for you tonight, Colman. Two Beings you have not seen in a very long time. Ten years to be exact … to the day."

What day is today?

"Guards please bring in our guests and bring them a seat to eat this delicious food."

The door opens behind me but the back of the chair is too wide for me to see around and too tall for me to see over, so I do a gait analysis.

[Alert. Two Subjects Approaching.]

[Subject One. Male. 6'5". 140 LBS. Gait Detected. Left leg: Injury.]

[Subject Two. Female. 6'4". 120 LBS. Gait Detected. Right leg: Injury.]

"My guests, welcome to dinner. We have been expecting you," Khan says, raising his glass.

I bring my head up and look across the table to where two malnourished Sivs stare back at me. It is obvious that they have not eaten in days, but they are not even looking at the food. Their unwavering gaze is penetrating deep inside me. Their eyes are extraordinary. The male has bright blue eyes with green specks and the female has light brown eyes with a gold rim around them. They both look like they could collapse just from the strain of breathing. Their bodies are covered in burn marks that have not healed. Tattoos stretch from the male's hands all the way up to his shoulders. He has a buzz cut and I guess he is ex-military. He has not shaved but his prominent cheekbones poke out from under his beard. The female's hair ragged, and her arms are that of a drug junkie. All over, there are unhealed spots where she has been jabbed with needles. Her skin looks like it has been draped over a skeleton. She is 6'3" for Spike-sake; she should be at least 170 pounds. Both of them are wearing sacks over their bodies. They do not look presentable but the way they hold themselves portrays that, inexplicably, they still have a sense of dignity.

I have been studying faces and emotions all my life and, in the female, I can see a combination of pride, determination, and one more thing ... what is the third thing? It is not lust, that's for certain. She is looking at me like she wants to make sure that what she is seeing is real. There is a combination of empathy, fear, persistence, hope, joy, forgiveness. That's not romantic love, is it?

"Please sit down," I say, gesturing to the table. I feel uncomfortable having them stand there staring at me like this. They don't move.

"Colman, do you notice anything unusual about these two?"

"Is this a publicity stunt? Are you bringing in impoverished Sivs to feed now?" I whisper, leaning closer to Khan.

"Take a closer look," he responds.

I do. The Sivs are standing at attention but the male wobbles a little bit. The Guard who brought them in pulls out a syringe and jabs it into his neck. He immediately regains his balance and his entire face relaxes. Their eyes still have not strayed from mine. *This is a publicity stunt.* Okay, I know the drill.

"You there," I say as I point to a cameraman "Come over to get our picture."

Khan starts laughing and then I start laughing because I am just so confused. *If he is not going to be a good host then I shall.* I stand up from the table and begin to walk around to greet them when Khan interjects.

"Remember you two - no touching."

They nod.

"How are you, guys?" I say. "Obviously, you know my name but what are yours?"

The female opens her mouth and looks to Khan. His smile gets wider and he leans forward. It looks like he is egging her on, challenging her to say her name. She takes in a breath and then closes her mouth. Soon, I reach the other side of the table and the two Sivs have arranged themselves so that I stand in the middle of them. I guess the 'no touching rule' really is a thing.

"On the count of three, make sure we all smile!" I say. "One, two, three!"

The flash goes off so brightly that I am momentarily blinded, and everyone holds their hands up to their eyes. There is slight pressure on the bottom of my coat and it almost slips off me, but I pull the shoulders back up in time for it to stay on.

"Wow, okay. I don't imagine that picture turned out well. Let's all do another."

"Colman, please come back over," Khan orders.

"Do you have anything either of you want me to sign?" I say, ignoring Khan. These poor Sivs probably traveled a long way to meet me. They cannot even get a good picture or an autograph?

"No, Colman. You are done."

Fear emerges from the depths of his eyes and I think I understand why. These Sivs are probably patients from a psychological ward. That would explain all the needle marks and why they are in such bad shape. Khan is trying to protect me.

"It was a pleasure meeting the two of you," I say as I walk back over to the other side of the table. I expect them to leave but they don't.

"Colman, do you happen to know what month it is?"

"It's April."

"Very good! Do you know what day?"

"I don't really have the need to keep track of specific days; they all blend together."

"Shame, then I better just tell you. Happy Entrance Day, my not-so-little Spike!"

"Today is the 19th? Thank you," I say with a smile, hiding my confusion.

The Sivs smile along with me.

"And do you know why today is an extra special Entrance Day?"

"Is it because I am 21 years old?"

"Very perceptive, very good."

"Thank you," I respond.

"Now you will really surprise and impress me if you get this next question."

"Is this some kind of game show?" I joke.

His smile falters but then he regains it. "No, it's not. Answer this question. Do you know who these Beings across the table from you are?"

"Fans?"

"Not just fans! These are some of your biggest fans. I was talking to them earlier and there was no end to the nice things they were saying about you. Isn't that right?" he says as he gestures to the two of them. They nod in agreement and I look over expectantly, waiting for them to say something but they just continue to stare.

[254]

"Thank you, both of you, your compliments are well-received," I say conclusively. *Why are they not leaving?*

"Do you know why I brought them here today Colman?"

"Are they part of a charity or a wellness program?" I say innocently.

Khan bursts out laughing as little tears form in the corner of his eyes. I am told that when a Siv is overfilled with joy sometimes they cry. I do not know how they can cry when they are filled with both sadness and joy, but I guess this is what happens.

"Oh my Spike, this is amazing! This is perfect! Did you hear that you two? He thinks you are charity cases! How funny is that?" Khan says as he holds his stomach. The Country Guards and the cameramen are joining in the festivities. The only people not smiling are myself and these two Sivs. However, they direct their completely unwavering attention from me to him. His face drops and his fit of laughter subsides. He looks disgusted.

"Poor sports, I am sorry about this," he says to the two of them.

"What is going on?" I say impatiently. I feel like there's a joke that I haven't been let in on. And it's pissing me off.

"I thought you would like to meet your Donors. Or, should I say, parents. Was I wrong?" Khan sneers at me.

CHAPTER 26

"Are you serious?" I say, aghast.

"Of course I'm serious!"

"These are my Donors?" I ask, dumbfounded.

"Yes." Khan takes another sip of wine.

"That is not possible. My Donors were killed in one of your chemical attacks. You told me so yourself."

He bursts into laughter again. "This day gets better and better! Wow, someone bring out the champagne. It is time to open a bottle or two."

"Why did you call them my parents?"

"They are, aren't they?" Khan suggests.

"I don't have parents. I'm a Spike."

"Bring them to their seats," Khan says as he points at the group of guards standing behind these people.

These aren't my parents.

"Bring out the food. They kept their end of the agreement," Khan orders.

Two Guards bring out two plates of food with a piece of bread, a glass of water, a slice of cheese, and one cherry. The two malnourished Sivs sit down slowly, nervously, like they expect their chairs to be pulled out from underneath them at any moment. They stare at the plates like hawks. When the plates are set in front of the two, their hands fly up from their laps and they both grab everything on the plate at once and shove it in their mouths.

"I hope one of the cameramen got that on tape. I will want to watch that later," Khan chuckles. He turns to me. "Colman, it is about time we had this talk. Now that you are 21, you are outside the terms of your contract with your Keepers – which means you are mine."

"That sounds so wrong…" I say to him.

"I was hoping we could start right after we finish dinner. I do not want to ruin a good meal together. Is that okay with you?"

"If that's what you want…"

"I knew you would come around!"

We spend the rest of the entire five-course meal in complete silence. Not that I'm the slightest bit hungry. I don't know those Sivs. They can't have anything to do with me. And yet, they're staring at me in a way no one ever has before.

It's like they care about me.

Don't they know that's grounds for Execution? Or maybe they don't care?

Maybe they would rather be dead?

Khan looks between me and the two Sivs the whole time. After they were done gorging themselves, they zeroed back in on me. I finish the mint ice cream to cleanse my palate, then push myself away from the table to show I am finished. One of the guards pushes me right back in. *Weird.*

"Now that we are all done, I was thinking we could relax in a different venue. Colman, would you mind if we went into my office so we can finalize this offer for us to work together in the future?"

"You mean this insane world domination idea? It's not going to happen. I will not be a part of it," I say strongly.

The "Donors" eye me with caution, but I could swear I see a little pride in their eyes.

Khan chokes on his wine then composes himself. "What a shame. Well, there are contingency plans for everything. Gentlemen, I think it's time to show this crew Alpha Ex, don't you?"

No one responds but suddenly my chair tips backward and I am dragged over the back of it. The same thing happens with the two Sivs and I do not even have time to respond before a needle pierces my neck and the world fades from view.

CHAPTER 27

I am hanging from metal chains in the middle of the Black Mansion's grand foyer. My feet are an inch off the floor. I wiggle to see if I can stretch so I can reach the floor but whoever put me here did a stellar job at measuring.

"I am going to cut to the chase," Khan says. "I am going to Execute your parents if you do not help me."

"What are you talking about?" I shout. "These Beings are nothing to do with me. I am a Spike!"

"I have kept them all these years, for this reason. Because no matter how powerful you became, I had them as a bargaining chip." He grins sadistically. "Now, it's time to cash in. You'll do as I say, or they'll be dead."

"I still don't get it. They mean nothing to me. No one does. I was built that way, remember?"

Khan's face is stripped of all emotion. I know this look, because I wear it all the time. He is receiving communication from his EYE.

"He's not playing around? Not a single one of his team ever let it slip? Interesting. So, what you are saying ... yeah ... so he actually doesn't know. And now ... yep ... would it make a difference long term ... okay but ... now is a good time?" Khan snaps out of his

Communications channel and returns his attention to me with a smile. "This is my fault; I thought you have been acting. I guess it is time for me to do a little storytelling. Are you comfortable ... ah, of course you're not. I don't know this whole story myself because I was not there on your Entrance Day but there is someone here who does," Khan says theatrically.

[Subject One. Female. 5'6". 142 LBS. Gait Detected. No Weakness.]

Molly. She is standing at the top of the stairs, swaying. Even from where I am swinging, I can see that she's horrifically bruised and still has blood dripping down parts of her body. She is escorted down the steps by two of the Country guards who picked me up in Jersey. The guards keep poking her in her back with the barrel of their guns and when she finally looks at me swinging there, she starts sobbing.

Here we go.

"Colman ... I ... I ... I ... am ... so, so ... so sorry..." she wails.

Khan walks over to Molly and gives her a reassuring rub on the back, but she pulls away like he has some sort of disease. He does not seem to notice.

"Calm down, Molly, it's ok, everything is going to be ok..." Khan says.

She brings her neck back, snorts, and spits a ball of phlegm in his face. At first, he doesn't even react because he is so surprised. It looks like he doesn't even know what happened. Then the flicker of a smile is replaced with one of the meanest scowls I have ever seen. He brings his fist back and sends it sailing horizontally across her face; her jaw cracks and she falls.

"Molly, sweetheart, stand up. It is time to tell Colman a little story," Khan says softly but I see him struggling to control his anger.

Molly rubs her face as she stands up. She has stopped crying and even looks a little pleased to see Khan's reaction.

"You have five minutes to tell Colman the story. You have been a good girl keeping it a secret all these years."

"You are a monster," she says.

"I may be a monster but at least I am not going to be Executed. Got it?"

Molly looks at him and nods.

"You may start. Do you mind if I grab a chair?" Khan says.

"Colman, I am so sorry to have done this to you. I should have freed you when I met you. Once I'm done telling you this you will understand," she says.

"You have just used eleven of your seconds. You have four minutes and forty-nine seconds remaining," Khan yells from his place.

"Colman, there is a lot that I am sorry I did not tell you before. By the time I realized what you were becoming it was too late. The Country would have Executed us instantly."

Molly takes a deep breath and begins. "On April 19th, 2040, the Country ran out of Nalgene-521 which, as you know, is a chemical weapon. However, it is only a chemical weapon when combined with Syrin and Carbon. It cannot be used on its own because it is too pure. Nalgene-521 is an ancient and rare stone that has to be distilled to create the potent compound. Since then, the Country has tried to synthesize artificial compounds, but every attempt has been fruitless. There is nothing any Keeper can do to make this compound again. On April 19th, 2040, Keepers injected what they did not realize at the time were the last two available vials of Nalgene-521 from their stores into a fetus that was growing inside a female which the Country had abducted from Australia. This female was known for her attractiveness and charm and was the last remaining Spike that could create offspring. The Country had created her, but she fled to Australia after she realized that the government was trying to weaponize her, just as they are doing to you."

"Four minutes nine seconds remaining," Khan interjects.

"This female was captured and brought back to the Country to enter into a breeding program with another Alpha who the Country had also created after the war. The male Spike was prized for his athletic ability as well as his charisma. He was taken from Canada. These two Spikes were the last of the first 'experimental race' that the Country had created before 2025. They were the very last two to have the ability to produce an offspring through natural means. The fact that Spikes can have offspring was wiped from the history books to make it look like the Country willingly decided to stop this process. They were embarrassed that they had blown their entire stores of Nalgene-521. They knew if other countries heard, the leverage of chemical weapons would completely disappear, and they would no longer have an advantage. This conceived Spike was, or is, you."

"So what happened to them?" I interrupt. "You told me that any Being even closely related to me was Executed."

"That is true. On April 20th, 2041, Khan..." Molly continues.

"Perfect, I love when I am involved in story time," Khan says as he smiles through his brilliant white teeth.

"...Khan found out that there was no more Nalgene-521. He sent a warhead filled with a different artificial substance and eliminated the ground where your Donors, excuse me, your parents, were being imprisoned. I was told that another State had committed this atrocious act and blamed it on the Country. I did not know whom to believe so I put my head down and did not ask any questions. You were in your Entrance Tube being injected with all these different fluids. There were so many scientists electrocuting you and cutting into your skin that I did not know what to think. I saw a poor, little thing like you, being prodded and experimented on without a single soul to care for you, so I volunteered to be your handler. I knew that I could protect you better than anyone else. I watched every single day as your body was used as a cutting board. Some days the entire glass tube would be red with blood. I saw entire chunks of your body floating in the chamber, just to see if the Nalgene-521 was helping you to regrow and repair the parts they had removed.

"This went on for ten years! Do you even know what that is like to see some little baby thrown into a tube of water attached to a breathing line and stored there for ten full years? It is unimaginable. On top of that, I knew you would never know your parents. What is a life if you do not have a family to live it with? I knew what they were planning for you and what your purpose in this world would be. I thought it was awful, but there was nothing I could do. It was not until April 19th, 2051 that I found out that previous tests with Spikes in your situation had failed miserably if their amygdala was kept in their brain. Many of them, traumatized by their past, killed themselves, or allowed themselves to die, rather than deal with the pain. A Spike couldn't become the perfect, emotionless killing machine with their brain still intact. You were the only Alpha Spike left, and they knew they had to remove yours to make sure you survived. On your Entrance Day, they drained the water, keeping you in suspension, and let you emerge for one breath of air only to put you back under to dissect your brain."

"Three minutes remaining! This is also my favorite part!" Khan shouts excitedly.

"Five minutes before the Keepers cut into your skull, I saw two Beings brought in the side door and brought up to the viewing platform with Khan. I got to the top where I used my Communication software to hack into the internal microphones and this is where I heard that it was Khan and your parents."

"Tell them what I told them! This gets me every time!" Khan shouts.

"Khan threatened us that if we did not keep quiet, he would Execute us before you even had a chance to live. We agreed." Molly continues, "I was assigned to be your handler and your parents remained in isolation. They have been kept in the Mansion for the last twenty-one years, in relative comfort as long as they do not upset the arrangement."

"So...wait, I wasn't created in a lab? I was created as a natural Being, even though I am still a Spike? And those people really are my parents?" I say, trying to process this.

"Yes, but that's not all. After I heard this conversation between them, I ran back down to the operating table where you were laying on the table. I saw that the Keepers had cut the line of connection between the brainstem, the dorsomedial thalamus, the entorhinal cortex, and were going to make the final cut between your hippocampus. So, before they could, I set off a medical alarm and the scientists had to stop. They ran out the room to see what the problem was." Molly starts to cry again. "How could they even think to leave a little boy of ten years old on a cold operating table with his head cut open?"

Is all this true? Did this really happen?

"I did not know what to do. I did not know how to repair a skull so I called one of the Keepers back into the operating room. I pretended that I had removed the amygdala but told him that I could not fix a skull. He agreed to fix the skull and he drained the blood and injected you with a chemical that would repress any emotional linkages left. He never even looked to confirm I had done what I said. None of these people cared about you! How can you watch a Being grow in a tube for ten years and then leave them all alone?"

"Then what did you do Molly?" Khan chimes.

"I made sure that you were back in your Tube safely and I left you to grow. I did not tell anyone that I interrupted the removal process."

"This means…" I begin to say.

"This means that you have your full brain still intact. The reason you cannot feel emotions is because the Keepers cut so many natural pathways in your brain and you would need a stimulant to strengthen the one existing pathway."

"Why are we here today then?" Khan sneers.

"I do not know," Molly says confidently.

Khan gets up from his chair, picks it up and brings it right across her back.

"Are you sure?"

Molly is on the floor, unable to stand.

"I will give you this one last chance," Khan says but Molly just looks up at him. Khan picks up the chair and he goes to bring it down again, but he suddenly pauses.

"Actually, it looks like we have a new story-teller. Molly, thank you but you can watch the rest from the sidelines," Khan says.

Out of the darkness, beneath the stairs, emerges a female Spike.

"Would you like to finish the story?" Khan smiles.

"Yes," the female says.

"Then let us reset the clock and start story-time over again!" Khan yells.

"Molly and I have been in communication, which was part of our agreement with Khan. She heard through her channels that the Queen of England had acquired a vial of Nalgene-521, which is required to restore your brain back to its regular functioning."

I look to Khan and it is obvious he is enjoying himself.

"This is why Molly set up the publicity tour in the first place—to try to coax the queen into giving up her vial."

"Tsk, tsk, so sad you did not get that vial from the queen," Khan says joyfully. "But even if you had, you need two to strengthen the existing pathway in your brain!"

The female does not say anything and looks at Molly who is staring right back. I think I see a small smile appear at the corners of her mouth.

"You cannot outsmart me, even if you tried," Khan says joyfully.

Something glimmers in the female's hand as Khan turns his attention back to gloating at Molly. She must see my reaction because her eyes go wide and she gently shakes her head. Suddenly, out of the darkness, bursts a male Spike at full stride. It all happens so quickly, and Khan sees it coming a second too late. The male springs forward and lands on Khan. The female breaks out of her chains and comes rushing over to me as the Country Guards scramble, barking orders into their wrists. Khan and the male are grappling but the male has him pinned to the floor. In the female's hand is a vial of blue liquid. *Is that Nalgene-521?* Even though Khan is on the ground, he looks over as his face is being pressed into the floor and he sees this blue vial. His eyes widen in absolute terror.

"The female, the female, grab her!" he screams, as the guards rip the male Spike off him. The guards reach the bottom of the stairs and are racing toward her, but she brings the syringe up to me.

"This is going to hurt a little bit," she says and jabs it into my neck.

Khan has completely lost his head and is rushing toward the female. She empties the vial into my neck and my body starts convulsing as I swing like a pendulum. A ticking sound slowly fills my head and my eyes get heavy. She drugged me. Khan tackles the female to the ground but instead of fighting back, the female is staring right at me and laughing triumphantly. Khan gets a few good punches in as his guards bring him back to his feet. He is now standing there panting but the male and female are recaptured and are brought to face me.

"Now, now, that was not a rational move, you two. What did you think that would even do? That is not going to do anything for him. You need two vials. Not one! I win again! Colman, Colman wake up, wake up, I want you to see me Execute the only people who have ever cared about you in your pathetic life ..."

I can't move. My body is still in paralysis mode as I barely hold onto life.

CHAPTER 28

My parents are recaptured and are brought to their knees in front of me. Khan sends a signal out of his EYE that he wants a sword delivered to the foyer, but Molly has maintained eye contact with my parents the entire time. The throbbing in my head has only gotten worse but even so, I wonder if they care about each other. *Do my parents care about me?*

"Khan, you are a coward and a liar. You are still waiting to see if he is going to join you on your irrational quest to dominate the world," the male says.

"Oh, please don't tell me that you actually expected me to reunite you with him. Do not use this to manipulate the poor Spike's emotions because, guess what, he still cannot feel anything. I knew you had that vial all along. I let you keep it, because I knew it would never be enough. You need two vials, you understand? And seeing as he is my prisoner now, I will never let another drop of Nalgene-521 near that boy. Your irrational quest of freeing him is over," Khan laughs.

I am still swinging while the ticking noise is getting louder; I have entered an altered state of consciousness. The physical sensation is similar to that of the moment right before I dip into a coma at night. I am dizzy, my vision is blurry; I cannot keep my eyes open. My tongue feels heavy; and my heart rate slows.

The jacket on my back has only gotten heavier and there is a pinching feeling coming from my lower back. I only see glimpses of the environment around me; my parents are still kneeling on the floor and Molly is being hoisted off the ground to stand next to them.

"Khan, you may Execute us but before you do, I have one final request," the female says.

"You're in no place to make requests right now."

"We have followed the orders you have given us without complaint," the male says.

"What is this request? Do you want food or something? Do you want to shower? I can tell you that definitely won't happen."

"No," they say in unison.

"Then what do you want? You already have my attention. There is no point in wasting it right now. Spit it out."

"We want to say goodbye to our son," the female says.

Khan pauses and he thinks about this for a while. Then, a large smile creeps on his face.

"Fine. I do not know what this will possibly do for you, but I will allow it."

"Thank you," they both say.

I am beginning to come back into full consciousness. "What is going on?" I say.

"Nothing to worry about. I am going to Execute your parents in a matter of minutes, and you will have to watch."

"I will not help you with your plan. I will not be used as your personal weapon," I mumble.

"How very wrong you are. You *are* going to be used as my personal weapon. If you look back to our last Encounter, you would be wise to remember that you cannot harm me."

My level of consciousness is flickering in and out. My EYE has a single red dot blinking in the center. *I have never seen that happen before.* I get a notification saying, "Rapid Release Contained".

Suddenly, the tops of the doors swing open and a guard carrying a very long sword walks down the steps.

"What do we have here? You two are in for a treat! They just sharpened this sword, so you are not going to feel a thing when you are Executed. Consider this my act of mercy for being good pets all these years."

"You will hold up your end of the bargain?" the male says.

"Yes. Whatever. Kiss him goodbye or whatever you want to do."

"Thank you," they say again.

"On second thought, I want to put on a good show for the Country. Guard call in the camera crews. Make sure they are set up for this."

I see the familiar blinking red lights enter the room as the Country Production crew walk in and start setting up. Khan is still speaking but I am having a hard time keeping my eyes open.

[Alert. Respiration Rate: Increasing.]

[Alert. Temperature: Increasing.]

[Alert. Blood Analysis. Blood Concentration: Increasing.]

That is impossible. I cannot produce my own blood.

[Alert. Perceived Exertion. Increasing.]

[Alert. Blood Pressure: 130/85. Increasing.]

[Alert. Respiration Rate: 20 Breaths/Minute. Increasing.]

[Alert. Pulse Rate: 140 BPM. Increasing.]

The alerts on my EYE keep coming but I still cannot feel any of this happening inside of me.

"Alright, the male can go see his beloved son," Khan snaps.

The male is shackled so tightly that he cannot stand up, so the guards hoist him to make his way over to me.

"You know what I do not understand though? How can you Love a Being you just met? You have seen this boy only through a screen and yet instead of food, clothes, or even a drink, the last request was used to say goodbye to him. You two are full of surprises!"

"Could one of your please hold his head up so I can look my son in his eyes?" the male says when he is next to me.

"No," the guards say.

"Please. This is my final request. Do either of you have a family?"

The guards are silent.

"Please, I just want to look my son in the eyes just once."

"That is acceptable. A soon to be Executed Spike just wants to see his son," Khan yells from across the foyer, where he is sharpening the blade and speaking to the cameraman.

"Thank you," the male says with relief.

Now he directs his attention to me as one of the guards grip my chin with his hands.

"Colman, I know you do not know me, but I wanted to tell you that I have loved you from the first day I saw you. I have seen you develop into an incredible young warrior as you have gotten older. I know what it is like to be kept all alone for such a long time and this is why I have to do this. Please always remember that I Love you." He kisses me on the cheek.

The guards let my chin fall back down as the male is dragged away.

"First batter up!" a cameraman says in a very official voice. "Tonight, we have Kendall Khan taking the first swing at a Spike's head. Let's hope he gets this on the first try, folks."

The female starts pulling against her restraints and is crying.

Why is she crying if she is a Spike?

"Khan please do not do this. Please, Khan, I love him. I will go first."

"Ah my dear if only … if only," Khan says.

The male looks at his Partner and mouths, "I will see you on the other side". Just as he closes his

[274]

mouth, after he bows his head, a metal blur comes arching through the air and severs his head from his body. The female screams and Molly starts to cry again.

"Kendall-baby is feeling good today!" Khan shouts and a few of the guards applaud.

The blood comes gushing out from his spinal cavity and starts spreading across the floor. I look at it and then look back to the body. The head is severed, and the eyes are closed. I wonder if he ever had an EYE like I did. When I received my first one, the Keepers told me that in the final moment of an Execution, the EYE will inject a small reserve of a chemical so that the Spike will be able to go in peace. It is a natural phenomenon inside an artificial frame.

[Alert. Respiration Rate: Increasing.]

[Alert. Temperature: Increasing.]

[Alert. Blood Analysis. Blood Concentration: Increasing.]

[Alert. Perceived Exertion. Increasing.]

[Alert. Blood Pressure: 150/95. Increasing.]

[Alert. Respiration Rate: 26 Breaths/Minute. Increasing.]

[Alert. Pulse Rate: 160 BPM. Increasing.]

The female is still crying, and Molly looks towards me. Something registers in her eyes, so I break contact and look back to the decapitated head. I saw the alerts but there is something happening to my face. I feel my altered state of consciousness retreat as my mind focusses and clears. Whatever was going on before is stopping. I taste iron and my nasal cavities are

[275]

filling with mucus. *What is going on right now?* I cannot take my eyes away from the fallen body and look to see where the female is now standing beside me.

"She has just as long as the male did," Khan says.

"Colman, darling, I want to say that I am the proudest mother on the face of this earth. You have become such an incredible, intelligent young Spike and there are no words to tell you how much I love you. I have seen all the natural gifts that we gave you, you have used every last one wisely. You treat Encounters with a sense of respect, you are kind and most of all you are a young man that any Being on this planet would be lucky to have in their life. Whatever happens tonight, I need you to know that I love you."

My head is completely stable as I look into her eyes. She must feel the tug as the guards try to pull her away because she stops, leans down, then kisses me.

"Please remember what I just told you, my darling. It is very important that you remember that," she says as she is pulled away from me.

The second she kisses my cheek my consciousness starts to flicker. My cheek is burning. My head feels hot now and Molly starts to talk again as the female is pulled away from me. She never breaks eye contact and is smiling.

"It was the night after Colman made the connection with Marist – after she burnt his hand. He went into his Tube after dinner to sleep. This was the night that his security guards were on call."

"What are you going on about now?" Khan groans. "You're next, sweetheart, but don't worry. I am sure when Colman joins me, he will not need you anymore."

The female beams.

"You might want to listen to this, Khan," she says.

Khan squirms as he looks between Molly and the female. Molly begins talking again. I try to focus but my body is on fire.

"A side effect of Nalgene-521 is that it brings a Being back towards their natural form. This means that it causes Spikes to heal naturally, instead of supernaturally. No natural Being is meant to heal overnight."

"What are you talking about, Molly?" Khan says nervously.

"The night she injected the first vial of Nalgene-521," the female whispers.

Molly smiles. "I *did* get the vial from the queen."

Khan's eyes look like they are about to pop out of his skull. "That's impossible," he whispers as he looks at me.

There is something going on with my stomach. I feel like I have indigestion and the bile works its way up into my mouth as I suddenly vomit. The ticking noise in my brain has gotten louder and it feels like my view of the world is getting clearer.

"I never agreed for the queen to Execute Colman," Molly says. "I agreed for the queen to capture him after I injected him with the first vial of Nalgene-521."

The guards around the room are moving closer, trying to hear what is being said.

"Shut off the cameras!" Khan screams furiously.

"This meant that she had to seriously injure Colman so that he would be unable to fight and would have to be taken somewhere to be looked after. I agreed that he could be studied if she protected him, but I never agreed that she could kill him. She said that she wanted to study you and use the designs to build a similar army. But not an army of people … an army of robots."

I am fully conscious now and my body is heating up. My muscles are flexing then relaxing, flexing then relaxing. I can feel the beating of my heart in my chest, hammering like a bird trying to get out of its cage.

"She said that human weaponization was too cruel a sport. But when I saw the carnage on the racetrack, I thought she had gone back on her word – indeed she had. I thought I was doing Colman a favor." Molly turns to me. "The night you Executed the queen, she actually was pulling a file out of her robes. It was a file to change your dwelling to an English residency. Khan came earlier but he did not notice that your hand was not healed. Khan also recruited Vassar and used her jealousy and anger to turn her into a spy for the Country."

I watch Khan, and I honestly never thought I would see so many negative emotions cross a Being's face at one time. Everything between fear, angst, and anger flashes simultaneously but I am still trying to figure out what is going on.

Khan flings down the sword and runs over to the control panel on the wall. I start to lower, and my feet reconnect with the floor. *I am so confused.* Once I am down, Khan takes the chains off me and hands me to the guards.

"That vial of Nalgene-521 that his female Donor injected," Molly continues, "was not the first vial Colman received in the past week."

"It was the second," my mother adds.

Molly looks at me. "Colman ... do you hear me? You believed you don't have a Pitfall, but it's not true. Your Pitfall is that your emotions can come back. It's a Pitfall for a killer, but not for a human. Which you *are*. Do you understand?"

I can only stare. *I am a human.*

"You don't have to be his weapon. You're free, now. You're just like us. Finally. Just like us." Her eyes fill with tears. "I love you."

I stare, as something pricks at the corner of my eyes. My parents said it, and it meant nothing. But now ... something strange grips me. I blink away the sensation. My vision bends. I feel like my heart is expanding in my chest.

I do not even have time to process what is going on; Khan races forward to the place he dropped the sword, picks it up and runs at my mother.

My life moves in slow motion. The ticking in my brain drowns everything going on in the world. Khan is ten feet away from my mother. My EYE analyzes the sword and it is five feet in length. My mother is not looking at him, she's looking at me. I see Love register on her face. Khan, furiously swinging the sword, wields it twice and brings it up and over his head.

My mother breaks eye contact with me and bows her head just like my father. The sword falls upon her and the metal passes clean through her neck like her body is made of nothing. Her figure remains standing and then begins to fall as her head hits the floor.

A red veil has coated everything in my line of sight. I cannot hear anything, and my vision is fading. My EYE is beeping "Rapid Release Uncontained" as I fall to the floor. Khan stands there over my mother's body and then spins toward me, but I cannot take my eyes off the fallen figure. I see his boots right in front of me and I feel the sword go through one shoulder right above my heart. He pulls it out and then sticks it through the other side of my body. I have no clue what is happening but out of my stomach rises something I have never experienced before. I look down at where I have been punctured and then look up at Khan in complete shock.

"A shame that I have to do this. We could have been a dominating force. The people who cared about you screwed up your entire life. I may not have you, but I am not going to let this minor setback ruin my plans. An army of Beta Spikes will do just as must damage as you could have done," Khan seethes.

He picks up the sword and I know what is going to happen. There is something deep inside of me that knows this is my Execution Day. I close my eyes and bow my head. The ticking in my head is unbearable now and I cannot hear anything other than that distinct sound. I wait for the blow for one second, two seconds, three seconds, four seconds, five seconds …

[Alert. Weapon Detected.]

This is it. I brace for the impact, but the sword falls shy of my neck and comes arching down in front of my face, striking the floor with a reverberating twang. The entire room is in chaos now. My vision is fading fast. The two gaping holes in my body are hemorrhaging blood fast. Why would they inject me with Nalgene-521 if they knew Khan was going to try to Execute me? This is causing me to bleed out faster. Two vials were also supposed to give me emotions, but I do not feel different.

Except …

Suddenly a sick sensation grips me. I think of all the people I've killed, a thought that usually makes me smile. Right now? I want to throw up.

Country Guards are firing their weapons across the room towards the other side.

I squint and see Molly running towards the darkness. Khan is sprawled out on the floor and there is a figure wrestling with him. It is much smaller than him. There is a rhythmic movement of the body. I open my mouth and just as I do, the figure wrestling with Khan turns to me. It is the little boy. I must be hallucinating. The boy turns and as he does, his body is littered with bullet holes. He topples over Khan's face as Khan scrambles to find a gun.

"No," I whisper.

No one can hear me.

The little boy stands up, unfazed by the bullets. My breath is caught in my throat. The little boy does not falter, in fact, he smiles and closes his eyes. Khan's bullet passes clean through his body, but no blood emerges from the wound. Instead, the figure of the boy fades away like mist evaporating off a lake. Khan stands there gasping for air, then arches his head backward and screams toward the ceiling. I can no longer kneel, so I fall sideways onto the floor as the chaos continues around me. Then, I get the one EYE alert I have never seen. [Alert. Blood Concentration: 40%. Decreasing.]

I smile. I was saved from a beheading by a little boy whose family I Executed.

He is me.

What does that mean?

I start coughing and see the still, lifeless, figure of my mother right in front of me. My parents were killed right in front of me. They just flopped to the ground. They were Executed because they loved me. I wish I could have loved them. I have seen this same thing over and over again. I have made this happen over and over again. They just flopped over. They did not fight, and they were Executed because they stood in my way. An Execution has never been like this. An Execution should not be like this. An Execution …

[ERROR. Abort Logical.]

An Execution … [ERROR. Abort Logical.]

An Execution … [ERROR.]

This will never happen again.

[System Malfunction.]

[Attention: Blood Capacity: 38%.]

[ERROR.]

[Invalid Code.]

My EYE blinks out of my field of vision. My right arm starts to twitch. My left arm starts to shake. My left leg begins to spasm. My right leg begins to tremble. My stomach clenches inward. My fingers curl toward my wrist. I see blood pouring out of gaping holes in my body as the blood fills in around my shoulders. What is happening to me? [Attention. Blood Capacity: 36%.]

I am on my side; head rolled all the way back – the veins popping out of my neck – and I begin to suffocate.

[Error.]

[Resuscitate.]

[Error.]

[Do Not Resuscitate.]

[283]

[Error.]

Today is finally my day.

[Safety Mode.]

[Alert.]

[Reassess.]

[Recalibrate.]

[System Reset.]

[Terminate: Non-vital Functions.]

[System Reset.]

[Conserve Oxygen.]

[System Reset.]

[Slow Respiration.]

[System Reset.]

No. This cannot be happening. I start to gasp.

[System Malfunction.]

No! I will not let this happen.

[Shutdown.]

My eyes are closing. My heartbeat is slowing. My parents are laying in their own blood, their bloodied and broken bodies engrained in my field of vision.

[Shutdown.]

This is not going to happen.

[Shutdown.]

[10.]

[9.]

[8.]

[7.]

[6.]

[5.]

Please, no.

[4.]
[3.]
[2.]
I will do anything.
[2.]
[ERROR.]
Anything.
[2.]
[ERROR.]
I will do anything for the people I Love.
[Invalid Code.]
[Initiate: Protocol Z.]
[System Erase.]
[Initiate.]
[Protocol Z: Initiated.]

I start drifting into unconsciousness as my eyelids flutter. Blood is spilling out of the gashes in my torso and every remnant of control I had left is gone.

[Initiate.]
[Protocol Z.]
[Erase Software.]
[System Reset.]
[Erase Software.]
[Reset.]

I'm staring at the ceiling. Water is pooling in my eyes. I can no longer feel any part of my body. I try to move my legs, but nothing is happening.

[Reboot.]
[EYE Malfunction.]
[EYE Restore.]

[EYE Recalibrate.]
[EYE Restored.]
Water in my eyes?
[Protocol Z: Initiated.]
[Restart Initiated.]
[10.]
[9.]
This is not some show.
[8.]
This is my life.
[7.]
Water?
[6.]
[5.]
Tears?
[4.]
Am I producing tears?
[3.]
Unless...
[2.]
Sadness?
[1.]
[Update.]

The End

--

ACKNOWLEDGMENTS

Thank you.

To my Teachers: Steve Arnett, the man who brought me out of the dark and into the light. You shaped so much of how I view the world today. There won't be a day where I will not hear you boom, 'Feighan, push!' from the second floor of the Armory; you are the reason why I relentlessly push today and I will be forever grateful. David McMenamin, there is a reason I overloaded every semester. The McMenamin minor was the best part of entire academic existence and why I continually question the world around me. You have changed my life only for the better, Professor; I have the tattoos to prove it and so I will not forget.

The Sages: Brian Graebe, for imploring me to assess my situation so that I may find God when looking at the best and worst of life. Celeste Wells, for the defining moment that ultimately, and literally, saved my life. I do not know if you saved my letter, but I think back to that day in Rhetorical Tradition every single morning. You are the reason I tell people I love them...over and over again. I will remember your kindness until the day I die. Lisa Vanikiotis, your lunch trip to Boston on that early spring day in 2017 was what kept me out of the hole that Celeste had pulled me from. The English language does not have a word to describe what your gesture meant to me. You have been an absolute gift to my family; I am honored that I know a Saint while they were on Earth.

The Characters: Colman Feighan, the inspiration. Happiness is limitless if you chose to act on it. Molly Feighan, the peace maker and the lover. Kendall Feighan, the attitude that you have given to life, you have so much that you can contribute to this world. Robert Feighan, dad and Master Bob. There is nothing I can put in here that you do not already know. I am so happy that I am your son. Stacey Vaughn, mom, for the years of guidance and support. You only have one first-born son. Stacey and Bob, you do not want to watch your children through a television screen. I suggest that you do all that you can to ensure that is an impossibility.

The Unconditionals: Gabrielle Downey, my life was changed for the better because of Boston Public Transport. You have talked me out of hand tattoos, remained my favorite dining partner, climbed mountains with me, and for some reason, still want to keep doing it. Thank you for showing me unconditional love, we will be in this together forever. Jimmy Cassidy, my brother from another mother. Keyes South will always be a blessing. You are one of my best friends and are the only person who read this book in its entirety before it was published. That is a gratitude I will never be able to fully formulate. Francine Almeda, my critic, my proof-reader, my tattoo-goer, and my accomplice. I am so glad I did push-ups in Keyes every morning and I am so glad that you were fearless enough to do them with me. You have, and will always have, a piece of my heart.

Jake Rosen, my go-to man and the founding member of the Super Sneaky Club who became my best friend. Thank you for your unyielding support and hope that if we get arrested for touching the Hollywood sign, it will be together.

The SQUAD: Tom Wimmers, Corey Peruffo, James Freiler, Jimmy Asselmeyer, and Steve Morrison, if there were a group of people who knew more about me than you do, I would be arrested. Bad Ass Bitches will reign forever. Thank you for having my back. I have entrusted the five of you with so much of myself and love each of you individually. However, the five of us are meant to be together.

The Influencers: Nancy Vaughn, Nanny, thank you for the gift of reading. I would not have been able to create this story without the dinosaur books you so aptly placed in front of me the second I could form words. Jim Vaughn, Sparky, for teaching me that listening is more important than talking. We have two ears and one mouth for a reason. Mia Fanto, my true older sibling. Thank you for the unyielding words and guidance that has helped me become who I am today.

For those who have touched my life in all other regards: thank you. I have been blessed.

ABOUT THE AUTHOR

Vaughn Feighan is a graduate of Boston College, having majored in Philosophy and Communication, combined with a minor in Psychoanalytic Studies, concentrating in neurocognitive theory. He has worked for the United States Senator from Massachusetts – Edward Markey; studied at the Suffolk County House of Corrections, a prison in the heart of Boston; and worked at a foster home for medically disabled and terminally ill children. Additionally, Feighan was an international model who traveled to London, New York, Los Angeles, Milan, and Paris, working with some of the biggest names in fashion.

The drive to become an author is attributed to the power of various forms of entertainment – books, magazines, social media, television, film – and its effect on the American culture. Given his immense travels to both developed and developing nations, he feels it his responsibility to write novels which will subconsciously change the mindsets of the audiences who read them. Currently, he works at an executive recruiting firm in Washington D.C. and is completing his tenth novel.